Reclamation
Legacy War Book 6

John Walker

Copyright © 2018 John Walker

All rights reserved. No part of this publication may be reproduced, distributed, or transmitted in any form or by any means, including photocopying, recording, or other electronic or mechanical methods, without the prior written permission of the publisher, except in the case of brief quotations embodied in critical reviews and certain other noncommercial uses permitted by copyright law.

DISCLAIMER

This is a work of fiction. Names, characters, business, places, events, and incidents are either the products of the author's imagination or used in a fictitious manner. Any resemblance to actual persons, living or dead, or actual events is purely coincidental. This story contains explicit language and violence.

Blurb

Humanity has unlocked another secret of the Orbs but it has put them on a collision course with their enemy, the terrorist group known as the Tol'An. As they race to collect another of the powerful devices, they must face another of their enemies, the cold corporate mercenaries known as the Kalrawv Group. Hidden away on an illegal mining facility, their purpose there can only mean one thing: they are trying to take the Orb for themselves.

But Earth has an ally in the Pahxin people and the battleship Stalwart is committed to assisting with the operation. As the two ships depart Earth, they head out to raid a planet which is known for destructive weather patterns. The unstable system holds the powerful secret from a long dead civilization, one which must be collected before either of the nefarious groups get their hands on it.

Prologue:

Ezria Tolva spent hours communing with the Trindisha interface, kneeling before it in solemn prayer. He remained quiet all that time, barely moving and hardly breathing. The wisdom from the device flowed over him, overwhelming him with inspiration. He knew what needed to be done, understood the next steps of their military campaign.

The locations of most of the Trindishas had been revealed and all he needed to do was get them. But who would he entrust with such a mission? His best agent was disgraced, languishing in a cell just down the hall. Tol'An men were loyal unto death but few of them held the sort of creative spark needed in order to pull off a complicated task.

Perhaps it is time that I give him a chance to redeem himself. Ezria did not tell Gizan he would ever receive such a privilege. He allowed the man to wallow in hopelessness, wondering when he might be executed for failing to hold on to the ambassador and human admiral. His failure cost the Tol'An much that day.

An entire base was destroyed, stolen files and countless deaths. After innumerable successes, Gizan finally faltered. And because there was a precedent to maintain, he had to be punished. Ezria felt proud of himself that he managed not to kill the man outright or to order him to commit suicide.

Even in his rage, he recognized he could not burn through talent like that so easily. He realized he might need him again at some point so he saved him, putting him away like a powerful weapon that needed recharging. By the time he freed the man, he would be ready to do anything to take back his name and honor.

That meant more to a man like Gizan than life itself. Even if Ezria had conceived of a suicide mission, he would still find the assassin eager to throw himself into it, anything to be brought back into favor. Rising from his knees, he turned to a nearby guard and motioned for him to follow him.

They paced to Gizan's cell and paused there, allowing the soldier to unlock the door before pulling it open. Ezria entered the dank, six-by-six cubicle and peered at his fallen champion, a man of great skill reduced to a huddled form on the plank attacked to the wall. *I wonder if the beast has been broken.*

The assassin wore tattered pants and was bare above the waist. Scars marred his torso, long white lines over his chest and stomach. Ezria knew there were many on his back as well. He'd endured great pain throughout his career. Each mark represented a sacrifice to the cause. His dedication never fell into question until he failed to deliver.

"Will you not kneel before your leader?" Ezria asked.

Gizan slipped off the plank without a word and knelt, keeping his head bowed.

"Very good." Ezria paced inside. "These accommodations are a far cry from the chambers you enjoyed before. After so many successes, so much passion and glory, you have fallen quite far." He clicked his tongue. "My disappointment was complete but what if I told you my anger has been dampened?"

Gizan remained silent.

"I would like to offer you another chance, Gizan. I have a mission which your talents used to be perfect for. Do you believe they could be again?" Ezria glared down at the man. "Do you feel confident that you can succeed after your failure? Do you still have it within you to be the hand of the Tol'An?"

"I do," Gizan replied. "I am ready to carve the enemies of our sect at your command."

"I see." Ezria sighed. "What assurance do I have that you are not a broken animal? A weapon that no longer has a charge?"

"I have cultivated my faith in the dark," Gizan said. "I have focused on my will, hoping for this moment. Now that it is here, I am prepared. Give me a task, I shall accomplish it. Whatever it may be, where I must go, I am yours now and always. Success shall be assured on my life."

"On your life." Ezria hummed. "It's good you brought that up because should you fail me again, I will have you stripped of your flesh. You will be roasted alive while being flayed. Do you understand the gravity of this situation? My need for you to accomplish this task? The Tol'An's very survival is at stake."

"I understand and accept the possibility that you've described." Gizan finally looked up at him. "You can rely on me. I take full responsibility for the last action, but the circumstances were not in my favor. This time, I will ensure they are. No one will stand in my way. If you unleash me again, then you will not regret it."

"Very well." Ezria turned to the guard. "Allow him to return to his chambers so that he might prepare himself for this mission. I will brief you when you've eaten well and stretched this cell out. You have today and tonight to recover. Tomorrow, we talk and I shall send you out to retrieve another Trindisha. Until then … enjoy your freedom again."

"Thank you, Master," Gizan said.

"Deserve it," Ezria replied. "Make sure you deserve it, Gizan, because there are no third chances with the Tol'An." He left the room, returning to the Trindisha interface where he dropped to his knees.

Communing with the devices brought him peace, gave him the confidence to continue the war against the universe.

There were many factions which would potentially rise against them. The nefarious Kalrawv Group would be in the way of their success this time. The Pahxin military would never help those scum.

It should be a simple slaughter. Gizan would be hungry enough to slaughter anyone in his path. Those mercenary fools would never stand a chance against true zeal. As his plan came into being, Ezria knew this was but one more step toward their domination of the galaxy ... one more motion leading to the cleansing of all filth in the universe.

He relished it.

Chapter 1

The Gnosis emerged from hyperspace, a short six-hour trip away from Earth. Captain Desmond Bradford let out a deep breath of relief. Scans showed everything was normal so nothing odd happened while they were gone. He looked forward to returning the two Orbs and having them back under lock and key.

When they left, an enemy force attacked Gamma Alpha. They did so while the military attempted to transport the precious Orbs to the Gnosis. Desmond was curious how it turned out and if they had figured out specifically who ordered the assault. Somehow, they coordinated with a Pahxin spy, a Tol'An operative who got on board.

There were a lot of questions requiring answers but as far as Desmond's mission was concerned, they'd been successful. They knew where to go next and better, how to interface with the Orbs properly in the future. It required some engineering effort, some construction, but they were well on their way to unlocking the next layer of alien technology.

The Pahxin starship *Stalwart* jumped into the system shortly after them, sending a message indicating they were fully operational. The two ships set course for Earth's orbit, prepared to report in to high command and begin the next phase of their operations against the Tol'An.

Agent Cassandra Alexander stepped onto the bridge, taking her station. She logged in without a word, but Desmond was far too curious to leave her alone. She'd been through quite the ordeal while they were away, having mentally delved into the Orbs along with Gunnery Sergeant Geoff Heathrow and Doctor Gil Vaedra.

The three of them wrote up their reports but Desmond wasn't entirely sure what to make of them. He assumed some of what they said had to be little more than hallucinations, odd sparks in the brain during the ordeal. Each described a scenario from their pasts, played out with minor changes.

Gil described them as locks, puzzles to solve so they could access the inner workings of the Orbs. Once they solved them, the three were able to ask questions of the devices, gathering information that was directly downloaded into their brains. When they woke, they could input their newfound knowledge into computers.

Desmond thought the whole experiment sounded risky. He doubted it would work when they took the devices aboard but when it did, he worried about the safety of his crew members. The three of them were put into a coma during the event and the medics had no idea what to do.

Once they regained consciousness, each of them appeared totally normal, as if the situation hadn't done more than drained them a little. After a meal and a bit of sleep, the doctors felt they'd be one hundred percent again. Some of them theorized they may not even have to go through the unlocking process should they try to access the Orbs.

After going in the first time, they seemed to have saved their password as it were. Desmond wondered if that meant they were forever marked by the devices, if they'd collected some extra baggage with it. No one could tell and even advanced Pahxin medical science could find no evidence of altered brain waves.

They didn't become psychic, but they sure as hell went through something crazy. Desmond looked forward to hearing the debates between the scientists about the situation. It was the sort of thing they lived for. After years of studying the Orbs, they finally unlocked something brand new.

Those who lived with the Orbs would certainly agree that what the three individuals went through was worth the risk. Desmond wasn't sure Cassie or Heathrow agreed, especially the marine. He complained about it the most of the three. Mostly because he wasn't even part of the experiment. He'd been in the security control room when they initiated it.

Commander Vincent Bowman and Cassie had become quite close. Desmond assumed she'd spoken to him if to anyone about what happened. He stood from his chair and joined her, noting how quiet she was as she stared at her screen. The terminal was running a scan of the Earth, but he couldn't figure out why.

"Welcome back to the bridge," Desmond said. "How're you feeling?"

"I'm fine, sir," Cassie replied, without looking up.

"No strange side effects or bad dreams?"

"None. It was …" Cassie shrugged. "Like nothing even happened I guess."

"Crazy." Desmond caught the vibe that she didn't want to talk about it. He motioned to her screen. "What're you doing here?"

"I'm checking to see if there was any sort of impact by removing the Orbs from Earth," Cassie said. "When I woke up, I had an epiphany. Our planet may have come to rely on having the energy present. If so, there may be some kind of anomaly to look at, a shift in temperature … anything at all."

"You're thinking the Earth might be dependent on the Orb?" Desmond asked. "Salina, what's your thought on that?"

Lieutenant Salina Gold acted as their science officer. She turned from her station, shrugging her shoulders. "It makes perfect sense to me. The thing's been there for generations … We don't even necessarily know for how long. Our weather patterns could be impacted among a dozen other things. I wish I would've thought of it."

"Can you help?" Cassie asked. "I don't have a baseline to compare to."

"I've got data from the last six months," Salina said. "We can correlate it against that and see what's changed if that will work."

"Perfect."

The two of them began to collaborate and Desmond returned to his seat. He felt better seeing Cassie interact with Salina, getting to work on something that kept her animated. The two of them dove into the technical details of their work so he turned his attention to Lieutenant Commander Zachary Caplan, the pilot.

"Good job with that course," Desmond said. "We got pretty close ... just as close as the Pahxin."

"I've learned a lot from them," Zach said, "but thank you. I was pretty proud of it."

"You should've been." Desmond smirked. "When are you going to let Deacon get us home?"

"When I'm in the brig or sick bay," Zach joked. "In all seriousness, he's been working on navs with me. He's just as good at it as I am at this point. I'm impressed with his numbers. I'd say with a little more flight time, I'd advocate for his promotion."

Desmond nodded. "High praise. When we leave next, we'll make sure he's on duty for the trip out. I think we're going to have a couple days when we get home. Will you finally take some time off? Leave the ship maybe? I heard you haven't gone to the surface the last four times we've been here."

"Maybe." Zach shrugged. "I'm just as good sticking around up here."

"Fair enough." Desmond checked his reports and saw a message coming in from Admiral Reach. *Impatiently waiting to hear if we were successful*. The request came through with just one word.

'Well?'

Nailed it. Desmond stood. "Zach, you've got the con. I'll be in my office. Let me know if anything pressing comes up." He turned and paused as his eyes fell on Cassie and Salina. They continued to work through their project, fully engaged. He left, feeling like things were well on their way back to normal.

***

Admiral Reach picked up the line the moment Desmond made contact. The older man's face appeared, brow furrowed in a deep scowl. A sigil appeared at the bottom right of the screen, indicating they had a secure connection and could speak freely. Desmond wondered who they were worried about intercepting the message.

The force that attacked Gamma Alpha? Or someone else entirely?

"Hello," Desmond said. "First off, I can tell you the mission was a success. We have the intelligence we needed and have learned the process to interface with the Orbs directly *without* going into hyperspace."

Reach let out a sigh of relief. "That's great news. Were there any complications?"

"From the moment we decided to move the Orbs," Desmond replied. "The attack at Gamma Alpha was a ruse to get an agent aboard the ship. They managed to inform the Tol'An of our destination then caused some havoc while we were in transit."

"How so?"

"They optimized our hyperspace component so the trip took far less time than anticipated. When we arrived, the Pahxin were engaged with the Tol'An. Luckily, our people gathered the information we needed quickly or we might've been in a lot of trouble."

"I see." Reach rubbed his temples before continuing. "So we know where the other Orbs are now?"

"Yes. Gil Vaedra and Cassandra Alexander will be offering full briefings when we get back in just under six hours now. We'll need to act quickly though. One of the Orbs is about to be discovered by the Kalrawv Group."

"Those bastard mercenaries." Reach practically spit. "Okay, so you're basically saying we've got our work cut out for us, right?"

"Don't we always?" Desmond asked.

"The story of our lives since we got the hyperdrive to work." Reach sighed. "Remember the good old days of ignorance and aspiring to the stars? Now … Now, we're deep into intrigues and politics. The Pahxin are about to establish an embassy here and we've been invited to do the same."

"That's good news." Desmond tilted his head. "What about the attackers of Gamma Alpha? Do we know who they were?"

"Mercenaries," Reach replied. "We didn't get any prisoners and they didn't bring along any identifying marks but after studying the tactics, our people have determined they belong to a group that doesn't really care who they hire out to. The Tol'An couldn't have paid them so that means we have a human traitor."

"I don't know how that's possible," Desmond said. "How would they even know to work with the Tol'An? How would they have established contact?"

"There are a couple different theories. One, they might have decided to take it upon themselves to work for the terrorists in the hopes they might talk to them later and seek some sort of compensation for their efforts." Reach shrugged. "I don't buy that one as much as thinking the agent got to someone and turned them quickly."

"It would've been really fast." Desmond frowned. "Maybe they threatened someone's family? I don't know. Who's looking into this?"

"I'm going to have Christina Dawson dive in when she returns to Earth. She's a good investigator and can probably turn something up quickly enough."

"Sounds good to me." Desmond considered the situation. If one of their own was causing trouble, then they would need to lock down their plans to gather the other Orbs. "We need to limit the number of people who will be involved in the next mission. Need to know only."

"I couldn't agree more." Reach nodded. "I'm going to keep it to you, me and Dulain."

Desmond fought an urge to groan. "Understood."

Reach chuckled. "You don't approve of him?"

"It's not that," Desmond said. "He's good at what he does and definitely enthusiastic. Honestly, without him we wouldn't have figured some things out up here. But he's definitely got an ego … and a lot of attitude. I'm not sure what to make of him but I do sort of see how he rose to prominence."

"Yes, he's a political animal *and* a doer. Dangerous combination if you ask me. And now he has more power than most politicians. If he wanted, he could start a war with just about anyone tomorrow. I'm glad he has enough sense to keep his ambitions in check and do the right thing."

"Do you think he's going to have something to contribute to the planning though?" Desmond asked. "I'd rather have Vincent involved if I'm to be honest. He has a tactical mind whereas Dulain … I don't have any clue where his head is."

"His primary concerns involve the dangers to Earth," Reach replied. "And he did graduate from a military school. I think you'll find he has solid insights." He chuckled. "Besides, if we tried to keep him out, he'd just find a way to sneak his way in. Believe me, inviting him keeps the AIA on our side and means they don't have to bug our rooms."

"Fair enough." Desmond frowned. "Do you think we should have the Pahxin captain involved? Ulian is a solid commander and if anyone could help us out, it would be him. I know he's faced the Kalrawv Group before. He might even know about the place we're going. I'd recommend him."

"Okay, I'll consider it." Reach's eyes narrowed. "You don't think he might be compromised?"

"Not a chance. If he were, he was in the perfect position to destroy the Gnosis and take the Orbs. He defended us with his own people. I would stake my life on his integrity."

"That's high praise." Reach nodded. "Okay, I'll let you know when you get here. Thanks for the recommendation. We'll talk again soon. Reach out."

Desmond leaned back, turning to peer out the porthole. He didn't have visibility to anything of interest on that side of the ship, just open space. The silence felt nice, the sense of being alone with nothing pressing for the next several minutes actually gave him the opportunity to relax.

His calendar would start filling up quickly. Engineering already put in a request to talk about some improvements. The damage done during the fight needed to be looked at. Security concerns had to be addressed. Someone from the Gnosis would need to be a liaison during the investigation into the person who worked for the Tol'An.

Desmond's world was about to be thrown into fast forward and he braced himself for it. That brief moment of silence was likely the last for quite a while.

***

They reached Earth's orbit and Vincent rushed through the hall, heading for the hangar. Cassie was already on route with Gil and Heat. All three of them were about to be inundated with questions from various people from scientists to intelligence agents. Their experiences interacting with the Orbs broke new ground and everyone needed to know about it.

Desmond allowed Vincent to join them, heading down to see if he might be capable of advocating for his people. He knew how doctors could be. When they got their hands on a new project, they sometimes forgot that their subjects required breaks and time to relax. God knew how long they'd be subjected to it, but he intended to be there to shield them.

Arriving in the hangar, the others were about to board one of the ships. Vincent dashed up the ramp, trying to catch his breath.

"Excuse me, Commander." Beaumont Dulain's voice made him straight up and he turned to look at the man. The intelligence director grinned at him as he stepped past before taking his seat. "I guess we're going to have a full load here. Christina and I decided to hitch a ride on the way. I hope no one minds."

Heat grunted from his seat near the front. "It'll be just as uncomfortable with or without you. These things aren't exactly the luxury liners I'm sure you're used to, sir."

Dulain shrugged. "We'll have to rough it."

"We'll see," Christina muttered. "If you're still good with that when we're half way down."

"At least we'll only have half way to go." Dulain shrugged before pulling out his tablet and staring at the screen.

Vincent nodded to Heat before sitting beside Cassie. She didn't immediately respond but stared into space until he leaned close. "Hey," he whispered. "You here?"

Cassie blinked several times, turning to look at him. She smiled. "Yeah, I'm good."

"You seemed a little out of it."

"Just not looking forward to what happens next." Cassie drew a deep breath. "Doctor Harper already left along with the others. They're getting the labs ready to start fabricating what Gil talked about. The Orbs will follow, and we'll get started later tonight. It's all very exciting … for someone, I'm sure."

"I'm coming with you," Vincent replied. "Hopefully, I can help you guys. I intend to stick around until they're done."

"Thanks." Cassie gripped his hand tightly for a moment before letting go. "I appreciate it more than you know."

"I understand they're going to be doing some serious inquiries." Vincent nodded in Dulain's direction. "That they're trying to pin down the guys who got that agent aboard and hired the mercenaries. You hear anything?"

Cassie shook her head. "I'm afraid not. I'm being treated as if I'm a little delicate right now. I'm surprised I was allowed to go to the bridge and work with Salina if I'm to be honest."

"Did you guys find anything?"

"Nah. It appears the Earth is not dependent on the Orbs after all. Scary theory." Cassie shrugged. "But it turned out to just be something to pass the time with. I'm grateful that Salina was kind enough to indulge me."

"Attention," the pilot's voice came over the speakers. "We are departing in ten seconds. Please be sure that you are strapped in. Thank you."

Vincent secured his safety harness and leaned back. Visiting home seemed nice but he knew they'd be too busy to enjoy it. He watched out the window behind Heat as the ship left the hangar end plunged toward Earth's orbit. For a brief moment, there was no sound ... Then they hit their entry window and the turbulence began.

Heat looked like he might fall asleep but no one else on the shuttle remained as calm. Beaumont stopped looking at his screen, gripping his seat with white knuckles. Much as the man liked to act tough and put on a show, he wasn't suited for field work, not anymore at least. His counterpart was another story.

Christina also looked cool as ice. She didn't even look up from her device as the ship started really bouncing, her face as placid as Heat's. The two of them were real soldiers, the kind who hit the ground and did dirty work on orders. Vincent had to admit he was more like Beaumont than they were.

When they were stranded, Vincent made his first real foray off the ship during an away mission. It was far more trying than he'd anticipated. He still privately struggled with losing Lawrence Gorman. The man sacrificed himself for the team, but it didn't make the situation any easier to stomach.

Vincent had led men into battle before but not since joining the Gnosis. Somehow, it was different when it happened on another planet. He couldn't explain why, he didn't specifically understand it, but having someone die away from Earth felt worse than losing those he'd lost in other fights. Perhaps it was the fact they couldn't recover his body.

A superstitious side of him stated it was horrible that Gorman had been lost on a foreign planet far from his roots. It was as if his spirit might never find peace being out there. Vincent kept the feeling to himself. Few people would understand. Perhaps not even the captain. As humanity pressed further into the stars, it would happen more and more.

And not necessarily through violence. Natural causes would eventually claim a life away from Earth. Perhaps part of the problem was the fact that the building acted as a temple to the strange inhabitants. They worshipped there and now Gorman was part of their dead race ... at least in body.

"You okay?" Cassie nudged him with her elbow and he smiled at her.

"Sorry, was I staring into space?"

Cassie nodded. "Yeah, you missed the whole trip almost." She gestured with her head toward Dulain. "He closed his eyes a couple of times."

"I'm sorry I missed it."

"You didn't miss shit," Heat said. "Er … sir."

"Surly as ever, Heat," Vincent said. "How're you feeling after your ordeal?"

"Fantastic, sir. I've never been better." Heat frowned. "However, if I'm to be honest, I would rather charge a machine-gun nest than go down there. If you understand my meaning, sir."

"I sadly do." Vincent sighed. "But it probably won't be as bad as you think."

"They're going to be thorough," Dulain said. "I would anticipate quite a few hours in the medical wing. And then there's the …"

Christina tapped his leg with the backs of her fingers.

"Oh … they're …"

Christina nodded. "Yep. They sure were."

"I see." Dulain cleared his throat. "My apologies. Carry on."

Heat shook his head. "Keeps getting better and better."

Vincent offered Cassie an encouraging grin, but he couldn't quite put any conviction behind it. Dulain made it clear what they had to look forward to and Vincent realized he'd made the right call tagging along.

Gil, Cassie and Heat represented three of the best crew members on board the Gnosis. They had survived the trip to the temple, saved several lives and continued to beat the odds on behalf of the Earth. Hopefully, their stint as lab rats wouldn't last more than a day or two but even if it did, at least two of them would be saved when the Gnosis had to leave again.

Never thought I'd be hoping for a combat mission so much, Vincent thought. *It might be the only thing that gets Heat and Cassie out of this situation in a timely fashion.*

***

Dulain stepped off the shuttle, taking a moment to thank God he made it without throwing up. He exercised every ounce of willpower to walk steadily, to avoid stumbling, much as he wanted to, and made it to the operations building of Gamma Alpha where he leaned against the wall.

Christina walked with him, barely containing a grin. He knew she recognized his discomfort, but she at least had the kindness to keep a jibe to herself. Did the others catch on or did she simply know him well enough to see the signs? Whatever the case, if anyone else saw his weakness, they didn't let on.

Nurses came out to escort Cassandra, Heathrow and Gil into the facility. That would be the last time Dulain saw them for a while. He needed to make sure they didn't give Cassie too hard of a time. He needed her back on the Gnosis for the next leg of their trip and didn't want her exhausted or out of commission.

"Christina," Dulain spoke quietly and she had to lean close to hear, "make sure they know to go easy on Cassandra. I don't care about the Pahxin or the marine, but our agent has to be ready to get back on that starship ASAP. Got it?"

"Yes, you're a humanitarian and you want me to make it clear," Christina replied. "I've got it."

"You know what I mean!" Dulain scowled at her. "It's not that I don't care about those people, but they're not directly involved in our actions with the Gnosis. Cassie has ingratiated herself with the staff up there perfectly. They've come to rely on her and if we need her to take control, she's in position to do so.

"I don't want to have to develop a brand-new asset."

"Understood." Christina looked away, clearly disapproving.

"Naturally, I don't want them to harm the marine or the Pahxin."

"Naturally?" Christina shrugged. "I was thinking you didn't much care either way.'

"That's not correct. I'm not a monster."

"You just become so focused that you sound like one sometimes." Christina stepped away. "Admiral Reach wants me for a briefing about an investigation into who betrayed us to the Tol'An. I'll talk to you later."

Dulain caught her arm before she could leave. "Look, I don't often say this ... I don't mean to be harsh. It's just that we're in a serious situation and it doesn't really cater to being gentle."

"I get it." Christina patted his hand. "Maybe I'm just tired of how we're direct behind closed doors or alone then dance around the truth with others like we're afraid something genuine might come out. You know I get it though. Just once, I kinda didn't want to go down a path where someone was practically expendable. Even if it's true."

"I can find another agent to do Reach's investigation," Dulain said. "You can take some time off."

"I'm insulted." Christina grinned. "Don't take my complaining as weakness or a plea for a break. Go do something shady, Beaumont. I'll be placating the good Admiral for a while and will catch up with you tonight for a briefing. Maybe we can find the asshole who sent that army here to mess with the Orbs."

"Good luck." Dulain watched her leave and considered his next move. He had a lot of people to talk to and little time to do it before the Gnosis left again. Reach invited him to plan their attack on the Kalrawv Group base, or at least how they were going to get the Orb back. He looked forward to contributing.

***

Cassie was surprised that the medical check-ups didn't last that long. The doctors had them run on a treadmill, drew some blood and ran some tests but after an hour and a half, they were sent to a briefing room to discuss what they saw again. Each of them recounted their experiences before Gil went about drawing up the schematics for the interface device.

After another two hours of conversation, they were given dinner and released just after eight o'clock at night. Cassie stepped out into the hall, nearly bumping into Vincent. He took her arm as she came out and she looked up at him, feeling dazed. The event had still been grueling, but her mind reeled at how suddenly it ended.

"You okay?" Vincent asked.

"Yeah," Cassie replied. "It's over. They checked us out … got our briefings … They already knew the star system … so I guess we're good. Gil's staying behind to work on the interface device with Harper, so we'll lose his company this round."

"Can we do that?" Vincent asked.

Cassie shrugged. "Thayne was there. He made the call. Once we have that device we'll have a huge advantage over the Tol'An. At least that's what they're all saying."

"You're not so sure?"

"No, but it's mostly just a bad feeling. Not based on anything real." Cassie smiled at him. "I'd love to get some downtime." She hesitated. "You ... want to come with me? I'm sure they don't need anything else from us until tomorrow morning. Even Dulain has enough compassion to leave me alone for the rest of the night."

Vincent was about to answer when his com went off. He held up a finger and stepped away. Cassie took the moment to lean against the wall, staring down the hall. Heat stepped out beside her, nudging her as he walked by. It drew her attention and she tilted her head, confused by the contact.

"We survived," Heat said. "You okay?"

"Yeah. You?"

"I've been through worse. You know what they say. Dread of the thing and all that." Heat chuckled. "I expected them to radiate us or put us through a freezer or something. This was a picnic by comparison. What're you two going to do now? I'm thinking of hopping down to the barracks and getting a drink ... or ten."

"I'm going to bed," Cassie replied. "I have no idea what Vincent's going to do."

Heat quirked a brow. "Maybe you both will?"

She scowled. "None of your business."

"Uh huh." Heat stepped away. "Have a good one, Cassie. If I had to spend a shitty day with someone, I'm glad it was you."

"Bye …" Cassie watched him go, wondering how he was truly doing. Gorman had been his best friend. Losing him clearly bothered the marine, especially when he talked about his experience with the Orb. She never thought she'd see the tough man emotional, but he very nearly broke down describing the event.

When it came her turn to talk about the training exercise, she held back. They pressed but she couldn't talk about it, not with any real detail. She had to dance around the truth to avoid revealing AIA secrets. The doctors weren't happy, but they had to accept it. Heat even backed her up at one point, reminding them of the term *top secret*.

Gil's description was far less personal than theirs, or at least the way he told the story it certainly was. He went through it without any passion, keeping his sentences concise and to the point. When he finished, he took a sip of water and made some notes before continuing on to what happened when they contacted the Orb.

I need to talk to Christina about what happened to me, Cassie thought. *She'll understand and more importantly, I can tell her everything. She went through it too.*

"Hey," Vincent broke through her thoughts, "I've got bad news. That was Captain Bradford. We're doing a briefing now that all the information's been posted. Admiral Reach, Dulain, the Pahxin Captain … It's a big deal. I … Looks like it's just us. Probably to talk about getting the next Orb."

"Undoubtedly." Cassie smiled, putting her hand on his cheek. "I guess I'll see you later then, huh?"

"I can come when it's over," Vincent offered. "If you don't mind."

"Ping me. If I'm awake, I'll definitely invite you." Cassie noted the disappointment in his expression. "Just swing by and knock. How long could they possibly go on at this hour, right?"

"Exactly." Vincent pulled her into a quick hug. "I'll see you as soon as I possibly can. Get some water or something. God knows what they did to you probably dehydrated the hell out of you."

"I will." Cassie waved at him and turned away, heading for her quarters. Exhaustion crept in on her. She hoped she'd recover enough to be ready for the next mission. Bouncing back hadn't been a problem thus far but after mentally touching the Orb and enduring a day long interrogation, she wasn't so sure it would be easy again.

Chapter 2

Gizan knew what would happen if he failed again. There would be no imprisonment, no admonishment. He would be publicly tortured to death to show the others what happened when one fell from grace. Despite years of service, even prior to the official beginning of the Tol'An, he too was considered expendable.

And that didn't set well with him. Yes, he understood the need to push for success, to ensure the Tol'An succeeded but operations involved fluid events. None of them could be predicted and therefore, failure was always a possibility. Killing good men because they did not always succeed made no sense.

How were they to learn from mistakes and improve?

Sitting in the prison cell gave him thoughts that he hadn't considered since long before he started working for the cause. He began to question the views of the Tol'An, and especially Ezria. Perhaps the man was not as wise as he had always believed. His arrogance began to encroach upon his sense.

Perhaps I am working for the wrong leader. Gizan didn't even feel treasonous considering such a thing. He wondered why it took him so long. He would do this job and return himself to the good graces of the Tol'An but he did not feel the same zeal he had before. Being cast aside so easily irritated him.

Gizan caught a transport vessel from a nearby Kalrawv Group base. They were sending in new workers to help with the mining operations and it was easy enough to sign up for the work. Only the desperate accepted such jobs because the conditions were terrible. He didn't care. He only needed access to the planet and everything else would be simple after that.

The Kalrawv Group had decent enough scanning equipment and he knew precisely how to calibrate it to find Trindisha technology. Once he gained entry into their control room, he'd locate it and call in his own soldiers to get it out of there. He figured there'd be a battle but despite having decent weapons, the Kalrawv Group soldiers rarely put up a real fight.

Gizan had killed countless of their supposed fighters throughout his career and he only encountered two that resisted with any real heart. Even they died quickly but he considered their ends to be significant blows to the Kalrawv military forces. Those who fought solely for pay never put forth the effort necessary to win.

He counted on the trend continuing when he arrived on their world. Security already proved to be lax when he snuck a knife under their noses. Gizan wore a tattered brown coat, threadbare cargo pants and scuffed boots. He looked like any vagabond miner, always on the move for work.

And the ruse allowed him through the checkpoint with hardly a second glance.

Other facilities throughout the galaxy would've caught him with it. Especially closer to the Pahxin controlled worlds. Out in the frontiers, the fringes of known space, rules, and those who enforced them, became lax. Gizan wondered if the Tol'An would fix that or if they would become just another centralized power, doing as they pleased while lining their pockets.

Cynicism challenged his sense of loyalty. As the shuttle put down on the platform, he began to wonder if he would ever trust Ezria again. If Gizan failed, it wouldn't matter how he felt. His leader would have him killed. But even if he succeeded, he didn't know how much longer he could remain in the Tol'An service.

What would I do with myself? Gizan dedicated his entire existence to working for the Tol'An. His zeal was never matched. Had he wanted it, he likely would've taken the supreme leader role but he chose to remain the blade in the night, the enforcer. His thoughts alone betrayed his station.

If Ezria knew Gizan was thinking such things, it would be grounds for execution. So many things led to death within the Tol'An. How did so many people sign up for the cause? Gizan couldn't fathom it but there he was, bound to them. Even if he left, how long would it be before some attack force attempted to catch up to him?

He knew the men Ezria would send. None of them could stand up to him but they would try. More lives thrown away, more men cast off for the vanity of a single individual. The Tol'An leader represented the real problem with the organization. They stood for something pure, but he took them down a dark path.

The doors opened and the foreman shouted at them to disembark. Gizan cast aside his doubts and concerns. He had a job to do and regardless of how he felt for the leader, he committed to getting it done. He stepped through the doors and followed the precession toward the admittance officer.

Soon, he'd have access to the communal quarters and then, be allowed to move about the station. The foreman likely already had a schedule in place for the new miners so Gizan needed to act quickly before they sent him deep under the planet's surface. It wouldn't matter too much.

He was in and the Kalrawv Group would certainly lament their lack of security by the time he was done.

***

Vincent entered the briefing room to find he was the last to arrive. Taking a seat near the door, he noted Ulian Hataran from the Pahxin ship Stalwart sat near the head of the table with Desmond to his right. Dulain was also there with Admiral Reach leading the meeting. He wondered why they kept the audience so small.

Must be more secret than normal.

Admiral Reach dove in. "I've sent each of you the intelligence we gathered on the planet you'll be visiting. The Kalrawv Group has set up an operation there to mine for resources. Note that they do not have a legal right to this location but it's far enough out of the way that no one would have stumbled upon them."

Vincent lifted his hand. "So we are not going to be opening some kind of legal dispute if we go in there and attack them? Just how shady is this organization? Thayne told me that they're basically a corporation and have been doing business for decades. How is that possible if they're always running around breaking the law?"

Ulian said, "The Kalrawv Group is a multilayered organization. Those at the front have offices on our home planet and do good business. They've sold starships, surveying equipment and countless other goods to just about every other organization in our alliance. However, it is also known that they have an underside."

"That commits crime," Vincent replied. "Correct?"

"Sort of," Ulian said. "The further out they get, the fewer laws apply. They bend what laws are in place just to the point of breaking. Employment records show they pull from outlaws, mercenaries and adventurers from around the galaxy. There's no shortage of people willing to do whatever it takes to make extra money."

Vincent shook his head but didn't say anything else.

"Anyway," Reach continued, "the planet is volatile. We'll be sending marines down to collect the Orb but know that on the surface, the weather is insane. Hurricanes, tornadoes … you name it, they've endured it. This should tell you how much the Kalrawv Group wants whatever they're mining down there. It's serious business."

"Must make them a fortune," Desmond replied. "So we're going to hop in, fend off their orbiting ships while our marines hit the surface, secure the package and get back to the ship. Seems direct enough. How much opposition are we expecting?"

"Severe," Ulian said. "They have committed a fairly large force to the area. This concerns me for multiple reasons. The first of which is they are out in the middle of nowhere so who are they expecting to show up and cause them trouble? Second, do they know there's an Orb there and are looking for it?"

"Do you think they want one?" Dulain asked. "I mean, governments start looking at these things with a greedy eye. Unless they kept it secret …" He paused. "I see. They find this one on the edge of space, bring it home and no one's the wiser. They have the opportunity to explore the benefits of one of these things."

"Exactly," Reach said. "But we still don't know if that's why they are there. Ultimately, it doesn't matter. We're taking it and they're going to let us. Ulian and the Stalwart will back up the Gnosis. The Gnosis will send down marines in power armor, which will protect them from the atmospheric problems."

"Did people once live on this world?" Desmond asked.

"Yes," Ulian replied. "Looking at the intelligence, my science officer states there was an indigenous people, but they died out. Possibly due to technology gone wild but she can't be sure without getting down there and performing several scans. I doubt we will have the opportunity. It seems we'll be in a bit of a hurry."

"Do the Tol'An know about this?" Vincent asked.

"We don't know," Dulain said. "There's no reason they should. Only a few people know about this planet and I've vetted them on our side … The Pahxin vouched for theirs. I think we're good. No leaks got out this time. Providing the mission launches soon, you shouldn't have any additional problems to contend with."

Vincent frowned. "But they have their own Orbs …"

"In which case," Ulian said, "we do not know if they can interface them properly. The Kalrawv Group may already be engaged with Tol'An combatants. But at least we know it was still there as of yesterday. Now, it's time to get out there." He stood. "I'll prep my vessel for launch and let you know when we can jump to hyperspace."

Desmond stood as well. "They finished going over the hyperspace protocols. The saboteur actually did upgrade the system. It's all above board and works fine. I guess he thought we'd be destroyed so it wouldn't matter. This means we'll be able to get out there faster … possibly on par with the Stalwart."

"Excellent." Reach nodded. "If there's nothing else, these men of action seem ready to take some. Dulain?"

"I'm good. I've got plenty to take care of here back on Earth and I'll let you know what we find as soon as we do."

Reach turned to Vincent. "Are you good?"

"Yes, sir." Vincent stood.

"Then Godspeed, everyone. Get that Orb. Make sure those mercenaries do not lay their hands on that technology. We cannot afford a third power to contend with in the middle of this conflict. The Tol'An is enough of a problem to keep our hands full without adding a bunch of corporate lackeys to the mix. Especially after all the reports I've read about them."

Vincent followed the others into the hall and stopped Desmond. "Why did we have such a small audience in there?"

"People are worried about a leak." Desmond clapped his shoulder. "Get some rest. We leave for the Gnosis tomorrow at eleven-hundred hours."

"Yes, sir." Vincent watched the man go and headed off to Cassie's quarters. He hoped she wasn't asleep yet but even if she was, the opportunity to put his head down for a few hours appealed to him too. The briefing had been short but what they discussed wore on his mind. It made him consider the dangers they'd be facing.

Some of their missions at least started out peaceful. This escalated before they even left. *At least we'll have some back up right off the bat.* He knocked on her door and smiled at the sound of footsteps approaching. Shoving aside all his concerns and worries, he let himself live in the moment.

***

Lieutenant Brent Fielding hated downtime, especially when it meant sitting around in a hospital. After defending the Gnosis, he received what could've been a career ending injury. If not for advanced medicine and some information from the Orb, he would've either lost the arm or never had full range of motion again.

The doctors were able to preserve his limb and he was already well on his way to mending completely. He'd even heard rumors that he'd be allowed to return to light duty soon. He pushed for it in a major way. Desk work beat lying around with nothing to do any day and he'd happily perform whatever task they came up with.

When Captain Darren Gabriel showed up to visit him, he had to fight back a surge of hope. The man gripped his hand in greeting. "How're you doing, son? You look a lot better than the last time I saw you."

"I'm feeling much better, sir," Fielding replied. "I'm off the pain meds now. I wish they would've had this tech the last time I got hurt. It's incredible."

"I hear you." Gabriel took a seat. "I'm here to ask you a question and I want an honest, no bullshit response, do you understand?"

"Of course, sir."

"Are you up for coming back to the Gnosis with me on light duty?" Gabriel held up his hand to stave off an immediate answer. "I could use you for the tactical operations onboard while the marines hit the surface. You'd be on coms, giving instructions and backup. You'd also be a liaison with the pilots who will provide some air support."

Fielding wanted to blurt out his answer but if he didn't show some signs of considering it, the captain would likely dismiss his enthusiasm. He drew a deep breath before replying. "Sir, they've talked about putting me on light duty. What you're suggesting is basically a desk job. I know for a fact I'm prepared to do that kind of work."

"I read that on your chart," Gabriel said. "And I'm happy to hear it." He stood. "The nurses are going to check you out in the next hour. I'll be back and we'll both return to the ship together. Welcome back to the team, son. I'm glad to have you."

"I'm glad to be back." Fielding resisted the urge to cheer. "Thank you again!"

"You're welcome. I'll brief you on the mission when we're back aboard the ship and you're settled in. We're leaving soon though so don't dally. This is a time sensitive situation and we're up against the clock."

"Is there any other way with us?" Fielding grinned.

Gabriel shook his head. "No, probably not. See you soon."

Fielding relaxed into the bed and stared at the ceiling. Relief made him smile despite himself. The nurses came to assist him with the sign out process. They gave him his clothes and he dressed for departure. Peering into the bathroom mirror, he frowned at the dark circles under his eyes.

I've had too much rest, Fielding thought. *I haven't slept or lounged around for so long in years. It was far past time I get back to work.* He couldn't wait to see the men and talk to them about their recent operations. He looked forward to the time he could lead them in battle again, get out in the dirt with them.

One step at a time. Fielding left the hospital to meet with Gabriel. He had a briefing to attend.

***

Squadron Leader Dennis Arden fidgeted in the hangar of Gamma Alpha, checking his watch every twenty seconds. He craned his neck, looking in all directions for the Pahxin pilot Dala Ahnshyr. They'd flown several missions together and intended to meet up before heading out on their next operation.

She seemed to be running nearly ten minutes late.

We're all busy, Dennis reminded himself. *She's not ditching me. She probably just got caught up with something.*

Pahxin representatives became more common within Gamma Alpha after the ambassadorial mission. The cooperation was fantastic, especially considering the Earth held two of the Orbs. The planet proved far more important and so it garnered better protection for the solar system.

Military personnel believed the Tol'An would launch another attack in the near future. It made sense. If they wanted to finish their goals, they needed to claim the Orbs and after failing to grab them in the last mission, the only chance would be to assault the Earth directly. Fortunately, they would have some serious opposition if they tried again.

"Good day." Dennis jumped when Dala spoke behind him. He turned, smiling at the blonde woman who looked incredibly severe in her black uniform. "I do hope you did not wait too long for me. They are locking down the entire base to transport the Orbs back to their cradles."

"No, it's fine." Dennis motioned with his head. "Come on, let's at least move to the side. The hangar can get a bit crazy sometimes. If we're near the wall, we won't be yelled at to get out of the way." He escorted her away. "How've you been? I'd hoped to talk more on the way home but it was so fast …"

"We are very busy. Planning this mission against the Kalrawv Group requires special care."

"Why's that?"

"Because they have excellent technology," Dala said, "but poor soldiers. They will be a challenge in the same way a child with a firearm is. They can still injure but they are not well trained. Of course, we might be surprised. If the location is as important to them as it sounds like, then they might have put their best me on the job."

"What're you recommending?"

"Our best," Dala said. "Get them out there immediately and have them hit the opponents hard and fast. Destroy their ships before they can launch fighters. Bomb the mining facility to eliminate soldiers. Then sweep the area with fighters until your soldiers are in place to claim the device."

"That ... seems a little harsh. What about civilians?"

"They are Kalrawv Group." Dala shrugged. "That means there are no civilians, only targets."

"Surely, they have normal people working for them."

Dala frowned. "Those who sign up for their service may not necessarily be the same type of criminal, but they know what they're getting into. They are outside the law. Much like the Tol'An. Do you have any idea how they have impacted our people? Made the civilian population paranoid for their lives no matter where they go?"

"These criminal organizations deserve what they get. If it were up to me, we would've disbanded Kalrawv some time ago and redistributed their wealth to the various individuals and families that were impacted by their greed."

They arrived at the edge of the hangar and Dennis leaned against the wall. "I didn't know you guys were so ... intense. Did you lose many people in the last operation?"

"Some." Dala directed her attention to one of the ships nearby. "Perhaps ten in total. They were honorable soldiers."

"I've seen how some of you fly. You don't use the most cautious of tactics."

Dala shook her head. "War is about winning. We lose soldiers in war but there are enough to ensure we achieve victory."

"Are you ... I don't know ... sad about it?"

"There is remorse, yes." Dala nodded. "We mourn those who pass. Do you not?"

"Oh, yeah, of course. I just ... I didn't know based on your response ... you know ... how you guys felt about such things."

"It's a matter of circumstance. We recognize the danger ... understand it ... but emotions are there, I assure you." Dala smiled at him. It made him feel better about the conversation. "War would be very difficult if we didn't have a pragmatic view of death. Those of us who serve, we choose to do so. This is not pressed upon us like the Tol'An."

"I get it." Dennis checked his watch. "Say ... we've got like ... two hours before we have to get back to our respective ships. Do you want to ... get something to eat together? The cafeteria isn't incredible but it beats a vending machine. And we can ... I dunno ... talk about something besides war and the mission?"

"I would like that very much." Dala gestured. "Please lead the way. I'm excited to hear more about your family and how you celebrate them on Earth. There are so many things I'm curious about. I hope you don't mind."

"Not in the least," Dennis replied, leading her out. The Pahxin may have been dramatically different when it came to their views on conflict and battle, but other parts of their lives seemed quite similar to the human way of life. The Kalrawv Group was a perfect example. Greed existed in every culture.

But that wasn't what Dennis planned to focus on that afternoon. If he only had two hours to spend with someone before they had to get back into the fray, he wanted it to be special. Or at least interesting. He wasn't entirely sure where he wanted to go with Dala or how far they even could, considering their culture differences … and living light years apart.

That didn't stop him from exploring possibilities, however remote they might be.

***

Chapter 3

Gizan received orders to report to one of the mine shafts north of the facility. According to the records he received, it would require an hour via surface railway and he'd be expected to put in a seven-hour shift. According to the foreman, he couldn't guarantee that's where he'd be the next day either.

They changed their roster nightly.

Inefficient. Gizan never thought of the Kalrawv Group as particularly thoughtful but as a money-grubbing organization, they should have at least kept a tight operation. To prove how useless they were, he departed the barracks two hours after lights out and wandered freely about the base, without hardly having to hide his presence as he moved about.

There were no guards and despite the fact they worked people around the clock, none of the services seemed to be open. The corridors around his particular crew were dead silent, making him wonder where they all were. Leaving the basic living area brought him into a more lively area where off duty workers gathered.

Men passed around drinks and shouted at each other, horror stories of their times in the mine. Most of them were likely exaggerating to impress the others. Their jobs were not glamorous and most of the time, they merely drilled the walls until they were relieved. No real effort was required by these people, not thought.

Anyone with hands could do the work.

He slipped through the crowd to the next corridor, this one leading to the living area of the actual Kalrawv representatives. Two guards stood at the passage way, barring his path. He sized them up, noted how bored they looked and decided on a crude but typically effective manner of getting them to move.

Gizan returned to the crowd and spoke to the bartender, letting him know he'd pay for everyone to have a round. Once that was announced, the people standing around became animated, shouting their appreciation. They surged forward to collect their free beverage and that's when Gizan shoved one miner into another.

The men connected and turned on one another, each under the influence of too much drink.

"Why'd you shove me?"

"I didn't. Someone shoved me."

"My arse. You shoved me!"

"I saw him," Gizan said, gesturing to the accused. "This guy definitely shoved you."

"Bastard!" A punch was thrown. The others turned to see what was happening. The fight grew more heated as the two wrestled each other to the ground. Shouts from the crowd encouraged them, egging them on to greater violence. Gizan inched his way back out to the edge, watching as the two guards left their post to break it up.

By the time they arrived, others had joined the fray. Gizan slipped into the corridor, leaving the conflict behind. He needed a security card, one that would give him access to other parts of the base. He knew someone would oblige and it was late enough that most of the most important individuals would be asleep.

If they bothered with cameras, they were well hidden. He didn't see any of the telltale signs of them, no bumps or holes in the metal. Perhaps there was no reason to be concerned about intruders. He found that doubtful considering the pay he'd been promised to fly out there but if they only relied on guards for security, it made his job all the more easier.

Gizan found a terminal at the end of the hall. He tapped the screen, bringing up a directory. It gave the room number of each of the people living there. Their titles weren't listed so it didn't prove to be of much use. He approached the first room and knocked on the door, scanning the hallway to ensure he was not seen.

The door slid open and a sleepy looking man peered out. He wore a pair of black pants and nothing else, his dark hair sticking up in odd directions. Squinting at Gizan, he cleared his throat. "Can I help you with something? Who are you? How'd you get in here?" He opened his mouth for another question but Gizan grabbed him by the throat, pushing him into the room.

The door slid shut. Gizan drew his knife and pressed it against the side of the man's neck. "I will kill you if you scream. Do you understand?" The man nodded. "Good. I have questions you will answer. Let's start with a simple one. Where is the highest-ranking individual of this base? Where do they reside?"

"Down ... down the hall ..." the man gasped. "He's ... in room ... sixteen ..."

"Thank you." Gizan sized him up. The man was roughly his size. "Where is the control room?"

"Why?"

Gizan tightened his grip and the man's eyes bulged.

"Okay! Okay! It's ... up ... the elevator ... in the ... north ... northwest ..."

"Very good. When is your next shift?"

"Five hours."

"Excellent." Gizan thrust the knife into the man's neck and brought him to the ground. He let go of his throat to cover his mouth, stifling his gurgling moans. After a couple of quick convulsions, the man went still, his eyes turning glassy. Gizan withdrew the knife and slid the man under his own bed then rifled through his clothes.

A proper uniform would get him far and after he visited the higher up, he'd have the key card he needed to access the facility infrastructure. Scanning for the Trindisha would be no problem and he'd have his people on the planet's surface in less than a few hours. He would restore his honor in the eyes of Ezria.

And then he could decide on his future with the Tol'An ... if indeed he had one.

***

Desmond stepped onto the Gnosis bridge and prepared to give the order for departure. Vincent was already there, working closely with Salina and Zach near the helm. He took a seat and left them to their business, turning his attention to a bevy of messages that hit his account in the last five minutes.

Admiral Reach sent an urgent message stating the Gnosis had full clearance to depart with personnel in place. No changes were required and any demands to the contrary could be ignored. This stood for all military and non-military crew members who operated aboard the ship and had been for some time.

That's strange. Desmond looked down and noted a message from Dulain and Doctor Harper as well. He checked Dulain's first.

Captain, please note that you have my full confidence and I look forward to hearing the results of your mission. Senior Agent Alexander is at your disposal. She is not required for further testing nor any other activities within Gamma Alpha. We will continue to conduct the investigation on Earth into the human traitor without her participation. Thank you.

Desmond scowled at the screen, but he figured out what was going on. When he clicked Doctor Harper's message, it didn't surprise him in the least.

Captain, I must strongly protest the departure of Senior Agent Alexander. While many of our tests were accomplished during that one afternoon, we have many more to explore, not all of which have been devised. Cassandra has performed this procedure two times, that makes her unique to the other test subjects.

Please reconsider taking her on this next mission and leave her in the care of Gamma Alpha researchers. There's a great deal we can learn from her. I'm sure you understand and will make this adjustment immediately.

Desmond was surprised both Dulain and Reach supported Cassie going on the mission. Technically speaking, she probably wasn't entirely necessary. The mission primarily involved military action, all combat for the most part. She could help with scans, of course ... locating the Orb potentially but so could Salina.

Yet her superior and Desmond's direct commander defied Harper.

Reach and Dulain probably see they have plenty on their plate without messing with Cassie. I wish I could believe Dulain was being wholly altruistic toward his agent. I'm sure he's got an ulterior motive. Why would Reach care? Must've been some kind of argument between him and Harper and he hates to lose.

Cassie entered the bridge and took her post. Desmond thought to mention some of what he'd just experienced to her, but Vincent interrupted. "Captain, we've coordinated with the Stalwart and our coordinates are laid in. We should arrive at roughly the same time as our allies and be combat ready in minutes."

"Excellent." Desmond turned. "Cassie, will you be able to locate the Orb when we arrive?"

"I'll work with the science officer on the Stalwart," Cassie said. "I'm assuming Salina will be too busy with the operation to do much in that regard?"

"I will," Salina replied. "But if you need help, I'm sure I'll be able to pull away at least for a minute."

"Sounds like we're all good." Desmond patted the arms of his chair. "I've received clearance from Admiral Reach himself. We can depart orbit and get this party started. Take us out, Zach, and remember, Deacon's bringing us home."

"I doubt I could ever forget it," Zach muttered but it was clear he was grinning. "Engaging thrusters. Breaking orbit. Estimated time to jump point, thirty minutes."

Time to grab a third Orb ... and solidify the Kalrawv Group as a serious enemy. Desmond squinted at the screen. *One threat at time. That's all we can worry about right now. Especially when one enemy merely wants to line their pockets while the other is intent on destroying civilization as we know it.*

***

Ulian checked how long it would take to arrive at their destination before turning to his first officer, Morala Crelden. She was absorbed in a report, reading intently. They went through the intel on the attack together, collaborating on what they felt might be the greatest challenges when it came to the conflict.

The information they received from long range probes from their people suggested a decent sized force, both ships and personnel. Several civilians were likely present, mostly prospectors and miners desperate for a big payout. The Kalrawv

Group paid well but were generally known for poor working conditions.

Morala worked out the attack plan with a few modifications from Ulian. Her initial recommendation didn't take into consideration the civilians and called for bombarding the surface as soon as they arrived to make an easier approach for the ground forces. Her rationale came down to the importance of getting the Trindisha.

Ulian didn't accept they needed to do so at any cost. Instead of hitting the surface, he recommended they engage the fleet above the planet, attack the fighters and let the superior training of the human marines take care of the Kalrawv security forces. They would be no match for the power armor, making it easy to preserve innocent lives.

He'd watched Morala grow as an officer, witnessing her rapid rise through the ranks. She didn't have anything left to learn about tactics or operations. All her lessons revolved around morality and not being rash. She still preferred to plunge into battle, spearheading attacks that would be far more effective with some subtlety.

Years of working together showed she was coming around but her mentality of putting her head down and plowing into danger still plagued her time and again. She needed to quell it eventually, definitely before she took command herself.

She continued to mature, honing herself into a solid strategist. It was just a matter of time.

Ulian had no problem giving it to her. However, it became apparent during their tactics session that she was somewhat impatient. Morala stated in her last assessment that she was surprised she had not received an invitation to apply for her own ship. Ulian had the unenviable responsibility to let her know he hadn't recommended her yet.

He worried it might cause a schism between them but after a conversation, she claimed to understand. Their working relationship didn't seem to suffer. Ulian decided that the best way to help her would be to give her the opportunity to lead more missions, give her advice but ultimately allow her operational control.

As they headed toward the Kalrawv Group mining operation, he would allow her to take on the action and only step in should his interference be required. He doubted it would be. Despite her impulsiveness, she was a quick-witted officer. The plan they agreed on held a high probability of success, especially with the Earth ship taking on the ground duties.

This left the Stalwart to worry about capital ships and fighters.

"Captain," Morala broke his thoughts, "we're approaching our destination. Emerging from hyperspace in less than five minutes."

"Thank you." Ulian turned to Erda Walar, their pilot. "Will we …" He paused and turned to Morala. "I believe this is your operation, Commander. Please. Do the honors."

"Thank you." Morala grinned but mastered herself quickly. "Erda, have you projected our exact entry point yet?"

"Yes, ma'am. We are right on target from departure. The Earth vessel should be in for the same. Intelligence suggests we will be less than ten-thousand kilometers from striking distance of the enemy. A quick thruster burst should put us in extreme range for targeting. I've taken the liberty of plotting that course and sent it to your console."

"I'll review it presently but plan on that action for now." Morala turned to her monitor and nodded a moment later. "This is a solid plan. Viran, I want a full sector scan the moment we emerge. Get me all data on any ships in the system, even those at the extreme edges. I want to know precisely what we're dealing with."

Viran Des worked as their technical officer and proved to be one of the finest Ulian ever worked with. She was a brilliant computer specialist and if she left the military, she'd have an incredible career in the private sector. As it was, the

Stalwart got to enjoy her skills for a while longer and they were all the better for it.

"Kalrawv set up a jammer in the system," Viran said, "but I worked out how it works prior to our departure. I'll have the data, but it'll take a few moments longer than we're used to."

"Didn't you just say you understood their jamming technology?" Morala asked.

"Yes, but that only means it won't stop us from scanning. It will take a few moments to get through their security and get the data we require."

"Understood." Morala frowned. "Do what you can and if you can hurry, do. I'm not sure that the human technology will be of much help in this regard so we can't necessarily rely on them."

Ulian leaned close to her, keeping his voice down. "Don't underestimate them ... but more importantly, you can keep that second part of the thought process to yourself. Distrust the technology, absolutely, but the rest of the bridge doesn't need to know your thought process. They're believe you know what you're doing. Justifying actions can make them doubt."

"Thank you." Morala's cheeks colored. Ulian didn't mean to embarrass her but at least none of the others heard it. Furthermore, there was no other time that would've made her less unhappy with the remarks. Part of the learning process involved taking feedback whenever it was given. "We are emerging from hyperspace in less than thirty seconds. Erda?"

"Counting it down now, ma'am." Erda began to call out the numbers. Viran informed the ship of their imminent arrival. Ulian sat back to witness his officer's prowess and decide how ready she was for her own command.

There was a great deal at stake on that mission but he still intended to run it as routine. The worst thing he could do was make a big deal out of it, pushing his people to worry and cause themselves unnecessary stress. That was the road to mistakes and they really couldn't afford many this time around.

That's why he elected to trust Morala. The confidence it showed in the mission would bolster the rest of the bridge staff and in the end, they'd succeed. He had absolute faith in his people. They hadn't let him down before and considering the opposition, he doubted he had anything to worry about.

***

The Gnosis popped out of hyperspace, just on the edge of the system. Zach called out that shields and weapons were online. Salina reported their position and that the Stalwart was already there and powered up for battle. Desmond put a tactical display on the main view screen, showing the position of enemy vessels in the sector.

"Stalwart reports," Salina said, "they are prepared to engage. Their pilots are prepared to sweep the ground ahead of the marines."

Vincent added, "Our pilots are in their ships and ready for takeoff. I'd recommend closing on the planet before we launch the shuttles or the fighters. Save them both some flight time and fuel."

"Agreed," Desmond said. "Zach, plot a course for the planet and ahead full. Salina, are the enemy ships moving to engage?"

"Not as of yet, sir," Salina replied. "The Stalwart is making a move toward them though. It doesn't look like they intend to give them a chance to fire first."

"They're taking the initiative," Desmond replied. "We'll focus on our task of getting people down there to start searching for the Orb. Once they're in place, we can help. They'll do their job so we can do ours. Cassie, can you scan the planet? If you locate what we're after before we arrive, that would be a big bonus."

"I'm scanning," Cassie replied, "but the atmospheric disturbances are interfering. I'm adjusting my technique … but I think we're going to have to be closer." She paused. "I'm jamming all communications out of this sector. They can't call for reinforcements now. Hm. That seems odd. There's one signal that can almost cut through."

"I see it," Salina said. "That is strange. I'll try to isolate it and figure out where it's coming from. Oh. One of the enemy ships is hailing us, Captain. They've marked it urgent.

"Put it on speaker."

"Earth vessel, this is Commander Arnel of the Kalrawv Group defense force. Explain this incursion into our space."

"I'm Captain Desmond Bradford. We have business on the planet. Kindly pull your fleet back and allow us access to your facilities and we can avoid any form of violence."

"Don't be absurd," Arnel scoffed. "There's no way we're going to allow you to enter our facilities uninvited. You and the Pahxin military vessel must withdraw at once or we will bring you both up on formal charges. Clearly, this is an unauthorized mission and we will not be intimidated."

"We won't withdraw," Desmond said. "Please consider complying with our demands. I can't give you any time to consider it. If you want more, you might want to reach out to the other ship. Let us know if you change your mind. Bradford out." He cut the line himself. "Anyone surprised?"

Vincent replied, "Only in that they haven't found the Orb yet ... or even seem to know it's here."

"They might've taken it away already," Zach said. "If they found it that is."

"I don't think so," Cassie said. "I can't cut totally through the interference but there's definitely Orb technology down there."

"Good." Desmond nodded. "ETA to planet, Zach?"

"Eight minutes at present speed."

"That should be enough," Vincent said. "Permission to launch fighters and shuttles."

"Granted." Desmond leaned forward. "Make it happen. Operation starts now, folks. Salina, if any of those capital ships start our way, let us know. Otherwise, this is in the hands of the marines and the fighters for the time being. I hope they're all ready."

"Strange," Salina said. "That odd signal is gone. I couldn't isolate it before it shut off, but it definitely came from the facility."

"Maybe they did call for reinforcements," Vincent offered.

"Possibly but it's not like any of their other signals ..." Salina shrugged. "Not like how they just communicated with us either."

"That is weird." Desmond sighed. "We don't have time to speculate about that though. How's the weather down there right now?"

"Chaotic," Cassie replied. "When we first arrived, they were dealing with hurricane winds but they've calmed down.

There's a super tornado ravaging the southern hemisphere but that's nowhere near any of the inhabited areas. I hope our people can get indoors quickly. If we didn't have the power armor, the surface would be too risky to deploy troops."

"Good thing," Desmond said. "I'm sure they're thrilled to play around in the wind. I'm going to leave that to them. Gabriel and Fielding have that part under control. I'm more curious about what happens up here at this point. Salina, focus on that odd signal while we've got some breathing room. Maybe we can figure that out even while we're busy."

***

When Fielding arrived, the marines were in the hangar to greet him. They were far more welcoming than he anticipated, even going so far as to cheer when he walked off the shuttle of his own accord. He joined them for a meal and listened to their recent endeavors and let them know what he'd be doing on the next mission.

They expressed excitement at having a field officer in charge instead of Gabriel. It had been a while since Darren led troops in battle and it showed when he gave orders. Fielding itched to go with them, to don the power armor and hit the planet's surface. The mission sounded insane but thrilling.

Dangerous surface conditions could work for and against them. The enemy wouldn't take to the surface if they could absolutely help it, but the marines didn't want to be out there more than they needed to be. Once they entered the facility, the real nightmare began: differentiating targets from civilian and military.

Fielding arrived in the command center a few minutes before the ship popped out of hyperspace. The marines were geared up and ready to go, waiting in the shuttle. He ran a coms test and settled in for the operation. Gabriel gave him some space, staying out of the operations center.

"You guys ready?" Fielding asked. "Heat, you sure you're good for this?"

"Yeah, that wound's fine," Heat replied. "Besides, the power armor keeps it in place. I won't have any problem doing my job. What about you? You certain you can talk with half an arm?"

"I've got a full arm, thank you very much." Fielding chuckled. "We don't have any way to friend or foe those people in there so be sure to check your targets. Hyperspace is dropping any second and I'm certain we'll be launching shortly after that. Once we do, I'll do my best to offer guidance from here but I understand there's a lot of atmospheric interference."

"That means bad weather," Heat said. "For those of you who can't read officer."

The men laughed. A brief rattle took the ship as it emerged from hyperspace. Fielding noted they were to hold tight until the ship approached the planet's surface. *That's going to make the guys anxious.* "Okay, so we're closing in before you can go. I guess it makes sense. Don't want you flying around unnecessarily."

Fielding checked air support and they were also ready to go but on standby. Raptor squadron would bring the shuttles in and give them air support on the surface for as long as they could. Mustang planned on keeping ships away from the surface while the Stalwart engaged the bigger ships.

They didn't have long to wait. Fielding got the order that the ships were launching and he engaged the different camera feeds, bringing them up on his tactical screen. "Gillet's camera's glitching out. Can someone take a look? Please don't perform percussive maintenance on it. We don't have time for a replacement.

"I'm on it," Private Brock spoke up. "Um … looks fine. Hold on." A loud tap sounded over the microphone and the camera started working. "Better?"

"Did you hit it?" Fielding asked.

"I … caressed it," Brock said.

Fielding shook his head. "Yeah, it's back." He checked their distance to target. "You've got less than three minutes to touchdown. I've got you landing just north of the south entrance. Should be light security there and let you get inside in a hurry. Remember what we discussed. Do *not* go outside unless it's the only option."

"No beach time?" Anderson asked. "And this planet looks like such a garden spot."

"Yeah, no surfing today." Fielding paused. "You should be hitting atmosphere right about … now. Next time we talk, you'll be on the surface. Good luck, guys. I really doubt you're going to need it."

Chapter 4

Heat didn't have to push too hard to go on the mission though he privately wondered if he was ready. Not physically. That part didn't bother him. After losing Gorman, he briefly wondered if he had it in him to get back into the field. There was only one way to find out and as he sat on the shuttle heading for the surface of the planet, he knew he made the right call.

"Two minutes to deployment." The pilot's voice came through his helmet. "Get ready. The wind's pretty heavy guys. I'm really fighting the stick on the way down."

The shuttle bounced around, buffeted by the weather. It dropped and got knocked to the side as thunder and lightning erupted all around them. Shields protected them from the worst of the storm, but Heat had no idea how the miners were able to work in those conditions. Just getting to their various sites must've been a nightmare.

I hope they're getting some serious pay.

"Opening back doors." The pilot still sounded calm, hardly moved by the situation. Those guys had the real nerves of steel. Marine pilots didn't receive enough credit for their resolve. When they dropped the marines off, they had to go off and remain close by for a quick pick up but out of the way of the storms with only a couple turrets to defend them.

The doors opened. Wind rushed into the cabin. Heat's HUD showed that the temperature was thirty-seven degrees Fahrenheit with strong winds, heavy rain and lightning. He glanced outside and had to smirk at the accuracy. He was fifth up and disengaged his safety harness to follow them out.

The first men out dashed for the nearby facility. Heat took half a moment to examine their surroundings. A barren landscape greeted them, stretching out to nearby hills. To their right, the facility they needed to breach, to the left, absolute nothingness. The place was practically dead. The fact it had any oxygen at all seemed like a total miracle.

"Door straight ahead!" Brock shouted. "Stacking up!"

"Form a perimeter," Heat said, "while we get through the doors. We can't just breach. Gillet, you're on hack duty. Gor ..." He stopped himself before he finished the name. "Vine, get a reading on this place. See if you can figure out when this God damn weather's going to calm down a little bit."

The rain hit harder, lowering their visibility considerably. No one tried to hinder them yet and that bothered him. Someone had to have seen the shuttles coming down on a scanner. If not on the surface, then up above. The Kalrawv Group had a decent sized fleet up there. What were they waiting for?

Maybe they're not stupid enough to fight outside. Heat stepped over to Gillet. "Can you get us a scan of the inside before you open the door?"

"I'll try to tap into security ... but it doesn't seem they have a lot of cameras in there." Gillet glanced back at him. "It's possible they're right on the other side, waiting for us to breach."

"That's what I'm afraid of. Vine! Stop screwing around with the weather and find us another door."

"But what's wrong with that one?"

"It was too easy," Heat said, "and that reminds me of your mom. Get your ass in gear and find another door! Take Anderson and Kelly with you. We'll keep working here. Hurry up!"

The marines rushed off, keeping close to the building to avoid the worst of the storm. It seemed to be a long hallway, just big enough for some ten by ten rooms to line the walkway. He figured it must've been for storage of some sort. It certainly was far enough away from the center. The control rooms must've been in there.

Intelligence suggested they'd find evidence of the Orb in the computers or through scans. Since the Kalrawv Group hadn't found it yet, they needed to do some probing to figure out exactly where it was. Heat worried they might have to do some digging and if that was the case, they'd have to occupy the place.

Holding the entire sector sounded like a nightmare but with soldiers from the Stalwart, they could at least batten down the facility for a time. Then the real search would begin, and he didn't even want to contemplate how long that would take. Without any clue, without a direction to start, they could be down there for months.

"Gunny," Vine's voice broke through his thoughts. "We might've found another door … Yeah, it's a door. Whoa! Contact!"

Of course they'd find the action first. Heat grunted. "You guys got that? Report back, are you in control of that situation?"

"Four combatants!" Vine shouted. "They have some kind of beam weapons and they're taking pot shots from a window above us. We've got cover for the moment. Permission to engage?"

"Yeah, open up and tear them down. Those windows might represent an entry point. Be prepared to pop in! Go!" Heat paced away from the others. "Lieutenant, did you get any of that? Are you on com?"

"Interference … bad …" Fielding's voice crackled, garbled in some parts by the storm. "I'm … gain … working … should …"

"Damn." Heat sighed. "Coms are down with the ship, folks. Here's what we're going to do. I'm going to join Vine, Anderson and Kelly. We'll try to get in through those windows. The rest of you stick with the plan. Hitting this place from two angles won't be a bad idea. Once we're in, we'll meet up near the entrance to the center."

Heat checked his HUD, noting the wind was far too crazy to engage his jump jets. He had to hoof it, rushing toward the sound of gunfire. The distinctive sound of the marine rifles barked over the odd wheezing from the enemy weapons. Remaining close to the wall, torrential rain pounded down on him, cutting visibility even further.

Muzzle flashes helped light his way. Vine called out for Kelly to take a different position. A jetpack lit up, purple and gold in the gloom. Heat opened his mouth to tell him not to do it, but the wind already caught him. The light from his pack became a streak as Kelly slammed into the wall.

"Kelly!" Heat shouted, lifting his weapon to provide some cover. The private landed directly below the targets. All they had to do was lean out to shoot him.

An outline took shape in the gloom up above, someone leaning way out. Heat took a shot, picking up the pace. The shot caught the target in the side and they disappeared back inside. The weather cleared for a moment, revealing Kelly as he tried to shove himself to his feet.

Their opponents seemed to withdraw for a moment. Heat grabbed the Private and dragged him back to cover near Vine.

"You okay, Private?" Heat shouted.

"Yeah, Gunny," Kelly muttered. "Just dazed."

"You have got to keep an eye on the HUD, gentlemen." Heat turned his attention to the window and aimed at it. "These winds could've swept you away from the building and then you would've been done. How many were up there, Vine?"

"At least three. I killed one for sure. Took him right in the face."

"I got one too," Anderson said. "That one you shot as you arrived was probably the only one left. Their weapons weren't damaging the ground. I did a scan and I think they're sonic."

"What the hell would that do?" Heat asked.

"It could disrupt our armor," Vine replied. "You know, vibrate the metal until it breaks at the seams or something. If we're right about how powerful they are, then that's no joke."

"How would they ..." Heat shook his head. "It doesn't matter." He paused, noting that the wind died down to a breezy twenty miles per hour. "I'm going for the window now. Cover me, guys. I'll let you know when it's safe to follow. We need to secure the area then head for the front."

Heat engaged his pack and flew toward the window, keeping his weapon at the ready. He had to grab the edge and pull himself inside, using the power assisted hydraulics to haul the armor inside. The strange wheezing sound erupted to his left. A blast struck the ceiling near his head. He dropped to his side and opened up, firing several bursts in that direction.

A man dove for cover but at least two rounds caught him in the foot. He screamed but it didn't deter him for long. He popped up, taking aim to fire again. Heat was ready, pulling the trigger just before his opponent could do the same. Three rounds tore through the man's throat and face, making his head snap back and his body go limp to the floor.

Heat got to his feet and scanned the area. There was a door to his left, a hall to the right and some chairs scattered about the room. It must've been some kind of break area, but it didn't make a lot of sense considering it was in the middle of what they assumed was the storage wing.

"This area's clear, guys," Heat said. "Get in here. Gillet, you ready to breach?"

"Less than a minute," Gillet replied. "They definitely stacked up on the other side."

"Watch their weapons. Vine will explain them." Heat aimed down the hall, providing cover for the others to enter. The Kalrawv Group prepared for their arrival, only not in the most efficient manner possible. They might be able to hold the door for a couple of minutes at most, so what was the real play?

They have to be up to something, Heat thought. *I guess we'll find out soon.*

***

Squadron Leader Anna Jager's Charger squadron flew escort for the Gnosis, maintaining a sizable perimeter in the event of an enemy attack. It was not the most glamorous assignment, but it beat having to brave the terrible weather on the surface. Raptor squadron called in reports that they had to stay above a certain altitude or they'd be torn apart.

The weather conditions made it both worse and better for the shuttles. If the Raptor fighters couldn't go down there, they didn't have to worry about the enemies flying around either. That meant more action above the surface, leaving the marines to deal with any ground forces, effectively on their own.

Flight Lieutenant Preston Everest closed on her left, tightening their formation. He'd become the new second for Charger after their last mission. Preston received the promotion graciously but with a lot of solemnity. They all appreciated Flight Lieutenant Frank Maze and his loss was felt by all the pilots.

Preston switched to a private channel. "Mustang Squadron's about to engage the enemy with the Pahxin fighters. I just got a private message from Lieutenant Alicia Quinn." That young lady also received a promotion, moving up from Flying Officer. Her bravery more than proved her worthy of the rank and she deserved it for all she'd done.

"We've only faced these enemies once," Anna said. "I'm curious how it'll go."

"You'll get firsthand experience I think," Preston replied. "Check scans ... Our four o'clock."

He indicated an area near the planet. Intelligence suggested the Kalrawv Group relied on capital ships to provide orbital support rather than erecting a space station. Pahxin authorities suggested it was because they intended to strip mine the place and wanted to remain mobile.

When the Gnosis first arrived in the system, the capital ships all appeared to be located well away from the planet itself, but Preston was right. A wing of fighters was definitely on approach in the opposite direction of their capital ships. "Something has to be hiding over there. Near the moon maybe? Or using the atmospheric interference to mask their sig."

"Won't be our problem yet," Preston said. "I'd like permission to engage these guys."

"Hold tight." Anna checked the scanner, noting they had six ships incoming, evenly matching them. She switched to the open channel, addressing Commander Bowman. "Sir, we have ships on approach to the Gnosis from somewhere near the planet's surface. We would like permission to engage."

"Granted," Bowman replied. "Keep them back. We're still trying to support the ground units and any distance will cut into our ability to perform scans or communicate. Good luck, Charger."

"You heard the man, folks," Anna said. "Follow my lead and we'll meet this threat head on."

She altered course, cutting down and below the Gnosis. The others formed up behind her in a loose vanguard. Scans came back about their enemies, offering a little insight into their capabilities. They were not the same types of ships they faced before but somewhat smaller. Engines suggested speed and their shields afforded a strong defense.

Scans didn't provide a reasonable look at their weapons though, and that's what Anna had been most curious about.

I wonder if these are the same as the ones flying around the capital ships. The Kalrawv Group were not a military. They didn't need to resort to specific models of weapons or vehicles. Instead, they could rely on whatever the best deal was or even go for completely different models based on situations.

From what little Anna knew of their organization, they built their own equipment and relied on internal factories to churn out their gear. She hoped that meant they'd do a great deal in an effort to preserve their ships but after their previous encounter with them, it was obvious they were nearly as zealous as the Tol'An.

Anna didn't understand what compelled them. It couldn't have been money, no one fought to the death like that over a mere paycheck and it wasn't patriotism. The Kalrawv Group didn't represent a country or world. The only thing left was some sort of threat, either to their families or their own lives.

Even still, those they fought on an earlier mission essentially sacrificed themselves out in the middle of nowhere. There must've been some alternative, something they could've done but without understanding their circumstances, it was impossible to guess. Maybe the Pahxin could help shed some light on what motivated them.

Some other time.

Anna noted they were less than thirty seconds from firing range. The enemy hadn't altered their course and continued charging forward, practically playing chicken. "Looks like we're going to exchange a first pass," she announced. "Reinforce your forward shields." She noted that Flying Officer Jonny Calloway was on the far left of the formation. "Jonny?"

"Yes, ma'am."

"Break formation and flank them. Give them a reason to separate." Anna scowled. "I'm hoping they don't have the discipline of an actual military. If that's the case, we'll have a distinct advantage when they get thrown into chaos."

Jonny swept out and away just as the first bit of ordnance started to fly.

Blasts from the enemy ships cut through space, bright green beams that remained visible for mere seconds. They were infinitely faster than Tol'An, near instant. Anna fired her weapons, discharging both beams and mass drivers. Her shields registered hits she didn't see, a half dozen before she darted past her opponents and finished the exchange.

Sweat covered her brow and she glanced at how her defenses were doing. Shields took a serious pounding from their strange beam weapons. Even with reinforcement, the attacks dropped them to sixty-five percent. What was worse, they weren't recharging as quickly as normal. Something about the attacks disrupted the generator.

"Did anyone else take any real damage?" Anna banked hard, preparing for the dogfight to come. She circled around in time to see Jonny make a run at one of the fighters, blasting it with a full barrage of cannon fire. The enemy's shields glittered green and gold, splashing with every hit. It made the pilot spin and dive, attempting to avoid further contact.

That would lead me to believe we can get through those.

"I'm down to seventy-percent," Preston said. "Seems like my generator really took a beating there."

Flying Officer Bella Graves confirmed, "I'm down to ninety and it's not going back up."

"No damage," Flying Officer Simon Gell reported. "Shields still at one-hundred percent and I'm engaging now."

Anna followed suit, coming around to find a firing solution on the nearest target. He cut to the left, banking to avoid letting her catch his tail. Pulling up hard, the inertial dampeners whined, and her body was crammed into her seat, nearly taking the wind out of her. She pulled the trigger, hoping to force her opponent back in her range.

The shots cleanly missed but the Kalrawv pilot must've thought they were closer. He pulled a barrel roll and ended up flying to her right, an easy maneuver for her to get into position. As she came around, she engaged her beam weapons, pounding his rear shields for a few moments before he pulled away.

Sparks danced over his hull, racing up the stubby tail wings and all the way up toward the cockpit. Parts of his ship began to move, rotating from the front to the back. *What the hell?* Anna squinted for a moment before she realized exactly what was happening. *Oh no.* She climbed half a second too late to avoid a blast that caught her on the bottom.

Shields dropped to forty percent from the blow. "They can rotate their weapons!" She shouted into the com. "Be careful of that!"

"They're just like our beam weapons," Preston added. "No recoil so they could technically fire from any angle they might have."

Anna spun into a dive. She'd lost her target temporarily but caught him on scans a moment later, breaking away from the conflict. "Where the hell is he going?" A thought occurred to her. "The Gnosis is jamming coms. I'm following this guy in case he calls for reinforcements."

"We'll hold it here," Preston said. "But don't go too far. He could be leading you into a trap."

Anna engaged her afterburners, dropping low. She started to gain but it would be a few moments before she could fire again. He was too far out of range for any of her weapons. If he was heading back for help, she had no idea how far he had to go. There were no larger blips on her scans still.

But either way, she'd catch up to him long before he passed the planet and then, he'd be done.

***

The Stalwart fell into position, charging the enemy ranks. A com signal came through from the Kalrawv Group. Ulian turned to Viran, who related that it was an urgent request for a parlay. Morala's eyes narrowed for a long moment before she finally nodded, gesturing to put it on the view screen.

A Pahxin man with dark hair wearing a Kalrawv suit appeared, his eyes wide with fury. He seemed to be trembling and his cheeks were dark red. He drew a deep breath before speaking, clearly attempting to calm down before he addressed them.

"What is the meaning of this invasion?" He demanded. "I've already spoken to your lackey and they directed me to you. I demand to understand why you are here and what makes you think you can attack us like this! You have no legal right to assault a Kalrawv installation! I can only assume you are a rogue ship!"

"Hold your tongue," Morala said. "We know this is not a legal mining operation. You're out here on the fringe, scavenging so that you don't have to pay taxes on whatever you find. This is strip mining, plain and simple. You have no right to be here, no permit for the action and no intention of telling anyone about it.

"We are here on business from the Pahxin government. You do have the right to stand down and surrender, but we both know that's not going to happen."

"Outrageous! Pahxin military thugs!" The Kalrawv man shook his head. "I will file a grievance about this!"

"Will you?" Morala asked. "On what grounds, exactly? You're destroying that planet. That breaks four different laws of our people, which your company agreed to uphold. Shall I cite them for you? Would you like us to transmit them for a refresher? In exactly thirty-five seconds, my ship is going to open fire. Do you surrender?"

"I do not!" The Kalrawv man shouted. "We will destroy your vessel and there will be no trace of you, or us, when anyone comes looking."

"We filed this attack plan with our government," Morala said. "They know you're out here now. If by some miracle you survive this encounter and destroy us, the military will know all about it. Your only real hope is to give up now and let us conduct our operation with your full cooperation."

"You weren't even going to contact us before you attacked!"

"I've dealt with you before," Morala replied. "I've never seen you give up yet."

"And we won't today. This is your grave, military dog!" The connection was cut.

Morala turned to Erda. "Do the honors of starting the engagement. Fire when ready."

"Yes, ma'am."

Ulian agreed with her assessment. She handled the dialogue about as well as anyone could, considering the audience. Kalrawv tended to only be cooperative when they were getting their way. Any other conversation ended pretty much the way Morala's did. They were like spoiled children holding handguns.

Willing to use them, not necessarily trained but incredibly dangerous all the same.

Kalrawv fielded eight capital ships in the area, seven destroyer class and one battleship. They held some potential for causing trouble, but the Stalwart was more than a match for them. The armaments on board alone were enough to devastate twice as many smaller vessels. Despite that, Ulian worried about tricks.

High-end weapons were Kalrawv's wheel house. They employed experimental equipment all the time, field testing them rather than wasting time in the lab. There was a good chance the Stalwart would encounter such things during the engagement, potentially something they had not accounted for.

When asked about it, Morala explained the obvious. They'd have to deal with such things as they came up. There was no way to predict the utterly unpredictable. So they charged in, targeting the nearest threats in the destroyers and allowing Erda to open fire. The first assault was a barrage of energy fire, cutting through space and flashing in the view screen.

Morala leaned forward, watching the screen intently. The attack took less than ten seconds to reach the target and shields flared so brightly, Ulian had to look away for a moment. Viran called out that they scored a direct hit. "Enemy shields on that vessel have dropped completely. They are wide open."

"Hit them again," Morala said. "All turrets open fire." She turned to Morala. "Has the enemy dispatched fighters? Are our ships engaging?"

"Yes, ma'am," Viran confirmed. "They have started the battle. Our human allies are joining them to assist." She sighed. "Ma'am, I'm picking up four larger vessels on scans. Possibly bombers but they're a silhouette I haven't seen before. It's not in the database at least. Isn't that illegal?"

"It is," Ulian replied. "They're supposed to register all new ships with the military before deploying them."

"They're hoping we'll be destroyed so it won't matter," Morala said. "Instruct our fighters to engage those larger vessels. I don't want them near the Stalwart. Erda, have you been able to get the turrets to fire yet?"

"Target is almost locked, ma'am." Erda clicked his tongue. The ship turned, moving fast enough to cause some discomfort on the bridge. Ulian held tight to his hand rests, waiting as patiently as he could. "Firing now!"

The turrets discharged, making a muffled whirring sound off to their right. Each shot made the turret whine as it charged up the battery and let the bolt fly. Twenty total beams hammered the destroyer, tearing through the hull and punching chunks out of it. The enemy vessel began to drift then exploded in a spectacular ball of blue energy.

"One down," Erda said. "Six to go. They're returning fire."

"This will be the test," Morala said. "We'll find out just how powerful they are and if we should be worried. Evasive maneuvers, Erda. Don't make it too easy for them." She turned to Ulian. "Opinion?"

"You're doing fine," Ulian replied. "At least as well as I would be at this point. Keep it up and don't let them have a breath. I suppose my biggest concern is their battleship … and why it hasn't engaged with us yet."

"Perhaps they have to charge something up."

"Hyperspace," Ulian suggested. "They might want to get out of here. The only reason I don't believe that though is the prize on this planet. Not the Trindisha … but the ore they're collecting. I think they'd be hard pressed to abandon it. Regardless of how obvious their end might be."

"Agreed." Morala turned to the screen, scowling. Beam attacks rushed toward the Stalwart, attacks from each of the remaining destroyers. They slammed into the starboard side, causing the ship to rumble and shake.

Viran cried out as she was jostled in her seat. The others fared better. Morala asked for a damage report but didn't get it right away. Ulian glanced back and saw the young woman shaking her head, tapping the controls. The attack managed to daze her, but she appeared to be okay.

"Looks like …" Viran cleared her throat before continuing. "I don't know how they've done this. That was concussion damage. They hit us with beams and it was like being rammed. It should've only damaged our shields … but instead, it didn't even scratch them. We have minor hull damage on several points along the side."

Morala hummed. "Thank you. Now we know. Their weapons are not entirely conventional. All the more reason to finish them off, catalog the results and report to high command about their efforts."

"One step at a time," Ulian replied. "Those bombers might even be worse."

"Get me a com link to our pilots," Morala said. "I want to reinforce the need to take care of those immediately. Erda, target the next ship and open up. Take another one out before they fire again. Vira, find out what it will take for repair crews to get us back up to one hundred percent. Move. This is a time for efficiency above all else."

Not exactly inspiring, Ulian thought, *but it could've been worse. At least she's got the whole conflict in her head at once. That trick took me a long time to learn. So far so good, Morala. I'm impressed. Keep it up and you just might have that command you're so desperate for after all.*

***

Chapter 5

Gizan found the officer in charge asleep in his bed. He crept up beside the bed, pressing his hand over the man's mouth before sliding his knife across the man's throat. The target woke, gurgling and struggling for only a brief moment before convulsing his way to a quick, painful death.

This man may not have been the highest-ranking officer in the facility but he held enough importance to be worth stealing his key card. Gizan rifled through the room until he found it and the man's tablet. Grabbing both, he paused before the bed, staring down in contemplation.

The facility didn't look like a normal Kalrawv construction. It was all too low tech and the amenities didn't match the typical comforts the decadent employees tended to require. Perhaps they merely renovated a research base, or it could've even been there since the previous planet inhabitants lived there.

Researchers would have killed for the opportunity to explore the planet, to catalog the wonders of the weather while excavating for buried treasure. Gizan doubted the Kalrawv Group discovered the planet on their own. They likely learned about it then kicked those out who got their first.

Typical. Gizan slipped out of the room and headed for the control center. He approached two guards standing in front of a door. They looked bored, hardly paying any attention to their duties. Neither of them even looked up when Gizan paused before them, within easy striking distance.

He held the knife backward in his right hand. Finally, his close proximity roused the guards. The one on the left looked up. Gizan lashed out and covered his mouth, slashing the other across the throat. Hands lifted to cover the wound as he wheezed out a wet gasp and dropped to the ground.

The other man reached for his gun but before he could clear it from the holster, Gizan slammed the knife into the side of his head, straight through the ear. The man twitched, eyes rolling back in his head before he collapsed to the ground.

His weapon remained lodged in the man's skull and he couldn't get it out easily. He took one of the guard's pistols then used the stolen security card to open the door, revealing flashing panels and tall computer banks. A man and a woman were at work, tapping at the console. They both looked in his direction, confusion washing over them.

Gizan didn't know if it was the fact they didn't recognize him or that he was covered in blood. They were nearly ten feet away. Their eyes moved to his weapon. He took aim. Both lifted their hands, eyes widening. He wasn't familiar with that particular gun, how it worked or what it would do to his targets if he pulled the trigger.

"Stand." Gizan spoke in a low, menacing voice. The man got up instantly, the woman smacked her knee on the console, wincing before she was able to leave the chair. They exchanged nervous looks before the male stepped forward, pursing his lips. His skin went deathly pale.

"Sir," he began, "my name's Dak and this is Jayla. I don't know what it is you want but please, do whatever you need to do. We won't stop you. We ... we just work here. Neither of us has any particular need to stand in the way of ... this."

"Are you not employed by the Kalrawv Group?" Gizan asked. "Because I was under the impression you people fought to the death ... too afraid of your supervisors to risk failure. Or in this case, capture."

Jayla cleared her throat. "I'm just a computer contractor. I don't have a full-time deal with Kalrawv."

"Me either," Dak said. "We're here for three months and then, the job's over. We go home."

Gizan wasn't entirely sure what to do with them. Normally, he would've just killed the two and moved on, but time spent in the cell made him second guess his typical tactics. These unarmed civilians would not likely cause him much grief. If he secured them, they could live through their experience.

Or at least have the same chance as any of the other Kalrawv representatives once the situation became dire.

Gizan narrowed his eyes just as Dak lunged for him, grabbing his wrist. The weapon was turned toward the wall as they began to struggle. A twitch of the finger discharged it into the wall and it wheezed, splashing a strange beam against the metal. *What would that have done to a man?*

Dak elbowed him in the chest but without enough force to hurt. Gizan kneed Dak's side twice then shoved him back, following up with a kick to the groin. Dak dropped to the ground but found an inner reserve of strength, throwing himself forward to tackle Gizan around the waist.

They both stumbled back against the door. Gizan brought the weapon down sharply against Dak's spine, hammering him three times before his grip loosened. Kneeing him in the stomach, Dak dropped to the ground and Gizan aimed the weapon at him, pulling the trigger once.

A yellow blast hit him, causing his body to tremble violently before he spit up blood all over the floor. Dak was dead in an instant. Jayla screamed, covering her mouth with both of her hands.

Gizan aimed the weapon at her, breathing heavily. "I was going to let you both live before this fool attacked me."

"I have no intention of messing with you, sir." Tears streaked Jayla's cheeks. "Please ... just ... What do you want me to do?"

"Come here." Gizan demanded. Jayla whimpered but did as she was told, approaching tentatively. When she stood in front of him, she began to tremble, tears flowing freely. He roughly took her by the arm, spinning her around so she faced away from him.

"Please ... Please don't ... Don't hurt me. I ... I didn't ... I didn't do ... anything ... to you ..."

"Hush." Gizan whacked the back of her head, knocking her to the floor. She landed on the body of Dak, making a sickening squish sound before falling unconscious. He stepped over them then took a seat, familiarizing himself with the controls. They were fairly standard, employing the same OS as other Kalrawv devices.

Gizan started to scan the planet for signs of the Trindisha technology. While it started the process, he prepared a signal for his Tol'An allies. By the time they arrived, he figured he would know how to complete their objective. Depending on what sort of fight the Kalrawv security forces put up, they may be done soon.

Several blips appeared on the scanner, drawing his attention. He tilted his head, bringing up the details of the find. A Pahxin battleship and another vessel entered the system and deployed fighters. He brought the silhouette of the second craft up, making his eyes bulge in surprise.

The Gnosis! He would never forget that ship's look nor the name. These two were responsible for his fall from grace, for all the doubt in his head. They pushed him to it and left with his prisoners. Their daring actions managed to end a scheme which would've brought both cultures to their knees.

Much as Gizan wanted to seek vengeance against them, he did not have the time nor the resources to do so. He needed to focus on the task at hand: get the Trindisha and escape. Kalrawv would keep them busy while he conducted his operation. And when his people arrived, if they were swift, they'd be able to get in and out under the blanket of chaos.

This might not be a bad thing after all. Gizan tried to remain calm. After what the two ships pulled off last time he met them, he couldn't assume they would be easy opponents. The only reason they could possibly be there was to take the Trindisha. In that, they were once again direct adversaries in a race against time.

Alright then. We'll match wits again, humans. Gizan directed his gaze to the window, peering up at the raging sky. *Bring yourselves down here and we shall see who is greater ... and who deserves the prize.*

***

Gillet struggled to disengage the locking mechanism on the door. Each time he got close to figuring out the code, it scrambled as if it was on some kind of randomizer. Then he realized someone on the other side was opposing him. They were keeping the door locked by changing the information whenever he nearly got there.

"Screw this." He stepped back. "Get to cover and rocket the hell out of it."

"What?" Brock asked. "Are you sure?"

"Yeah, I'm sure. We don't have time to play games." Gillet waved and shouted. "Fall back!" They retreated nearly fifty feet from the door. "That thing's tough so everyone, give it a single rocket. Should be enough to punch right through and get us inside. Plus, those assholes waiting for us will be in for one hell of a surprise."

The marines fired their rockets, sending them streaking through the air. They moved swiftly, defying the moderate winds and pounding their target, tearing a hole in the wall and knocking down the door. People screamed inside, shock and pain mingling. Gillet charged forward, shouting for his men to follow him in.

Wheezing blasts filled the air, the Kalrawv security team blind fired into the breached wall. Gillet returned fire, spraying bullets into the chamber not twenty feet before entering the building. Heat's voice came shouting over the speakers, demanding to know what just happened.

Private Erskin hit the ground to Gillet's left, crying out. Private Howards hit the wall just inside the breach. Body parts from their opponents littered the ground, though it was impossible to tell how many were dead in the heat of the battle.

Gillet took aim and shot at a target stumbling to the right, moving into the hallway. He caught him in the stomach. The blow made the man spin in place and drop to the ground, blood soaking the metal floor.

More chaos reigned around him, yellow energy beams slapping the walls and rifles barking as they blasted away. Gillet tried to identify another target, but the carnage seemed to be calming down. A couple bursts from his men made him twitch, ducking for a moment before approaching his two downed soldiers.

"Erskin," Gillet shouted into his com. "You still with us?"

"Yes, sir," Erskin muttered, shoving himself to his feet. "They hit me in the shoulder with that … that energy beam. It disrupted my circuits, but they rebooted. I seem to be fine."

"Run a diagnostic to be sure." Gillet turned to Howards and stopped before speaking. He'd taken a blow to the head. Blood and chunks sat beneath his helmet, enough that indicated he was dead the moment it made contact. "Jesus Christ ... Mark down Howards as KIA."

"What the hell?" Heat shouted. "What happened, Gillet?"

"We're inside," Gillet replied. "We're moving in your direction. Howards is down but we're otherwise okay. I've seen what those sonic weapons can do now. We definitely want to avoid contact with them." He looked back at Howards. "More than you can possibly guess. Poor guy."

"We've secured the area!" Erskin called out. "We're ready to move."

"We're on our way to you," Gillet said. "Coming up from your six so please don't shoot at us when we get close."

"Your stunt made the whole facility shake," Heat replied. "You might want to hurry so we're not fighting a pitch battle in close quarters. It won't be pleasant."

"No problem, Gunny." Gillet checked his ammo and led the way. "We'll pick up the pace."

***

Cassie grunted, slapping the console. Even though they were near orbit with the planet, scans were not able to break through the atmospheric interference. She tried a dozen different techniques to compensate for the noise, but they needed a booster on the surface to make it happen.

She even tried to hack into the Kalrawv network in an effort to use their equipment to help but they weren't broadcasting a powerful enough signal to maintain the connection. She needed the marines to get into the system. If she had access to their computers, if they were sending a strong enough signal, the planetary scans would be possible.

"Captain," Cassie said, "I need to send a message to the marines. Without their help, I won't be able to find the Orb from up here."

"Weather?" Desmond asked.

"That and more," Cassie replied. "The static electricity from the clouds alone is enough to throw our instruments for a loop. We *could* drop to a lower orbit, but I can't guarantee that will be enough. Really, it comes down to the marines."

"We needed to give them a clear objective of where to go," Desmond said. "Okay, talk to Fielding. He's got operational command of the mission."

"Thanks." Cassie contacted ground operations and the line connected right away.

"This is Fielding."

"Lieutenant, Agent Alexander here. I need your guys to take the control center down there to help me establish a link to their systems. The interference is too great for our scans to punch through."

"I'd love to let them know," Fielding replied, "but communications are down. Standard procedure at this point would be to find a way to connect up with us. In that case, they should already be on your request."

"Thank you." Cassie frowned. "So not even communications are getting through? We tight beam that too. Maybe our jamming is causing the problem. I'll look into it. Thank you, Lieutenant."

She killed the connection and moved over to Salina, keeping her voice low. "They can't talk to the surface and we can't deep scan either. I know we're jamming the system to prevent them from reaching out for reinforcements. Is there a chance that's impacting our systems as well? Some sort of anomaly due to that terrible weather?"

Salina sighed, wearing a perplexed expression. "I don't think so. Or at least, I wouldn't think it should. To be honest, we're treading on new territory here. It's not like we've jammed a whole system before. But ..." She snapped her fingers. "You know, I think the Stalwart is blasting the capital ships over there."

"The combination of all three?" Cassie asked.

"Maybe. I'll talk to Chief Webber and see if he's got any ideas about it."

"I'll see what I can do." Cassie shook her head as she returned to her station. "Though I've already gone through several options."

"We've got incoming," Zach said. "Kalrawv destroyer moving in from around the other side of the planet." He paused. "They're on an intercept course with us."

"I thought it was too quiet over here," Desmond muttered. "Bring us around and charge up the batteries. Full power to the shields."

"But if we have the shields up," Cassie said, "that's another layer of interference we have to get through. I can't scan through that."

"Then maybe we should get you down there," Desmond replied. "If you join the marines, you'll be able to do the scans from the surface, find the Orb and assist with its extraction."

"She doesn't have power armor," Vincent said. "And how would she get down there?"

Desmond turned to him. "Send a bomber. They're tough enough to handle that weather and better armed than any of the shuttles."

"Captain …" Vincent seemed ready to continue to argue so Cassie stepped in.

"I'll do it. But I have to hurry. If we're about to enter combat, I need to be off the ship before they get here and start in with the shooting."

"There you go," Desmond said. "She's ready for action, Vincent. See to it that the bombers are prepared to launch. We can have them come back up and help with this destroyer when they've dropped her off."

Vincent stood, moving to her station and leaning close. He kept his voice down, practically whispering. "You don't have to do this. It's not your job. We can … send a technician. Seriously. Don't go."

"I'm the one who knows what to look for when it comes to the Orb," Cassie said. "There's not enough time to explain it to someone else. It's not like they can be on the com."

"I don't like it."

"I know." Cassie smiled as she stood. "I'll be back soon. You'd better contact Rhino and let them know to be ready." She headed to the elevator. "Captain, I'll try to establish communications as soon as I can. Good luck up here." She waved at Vincent as the doors closed.

She headed down to get geared up for the trip and drew a deep breath, steadying herself. Vincent was right, she didn't have to go. She could've even pulled rank if necessary. There wasn't anyone else who could do it. Without heading to the planet, they delayed the mission until the marines secured the facility.

That required time they didn't have. *So now I get to see how bad weather can really get.* Cassie smirked. *I doubt I'll complain much about rain back home after this. Gotta take the small things, right?*

***

Squadron Leader Nolan Coplan and his bomber unit went on standby the moment the Gnosis emerged from hyperspace. He didn't expect to launch, not after the briefing he attended but when he received an urgent communication request from the bridge, he figured the battlefield must've changed.

He established the link to Commander Bowman. "Yes, sir?"

"Hi Nolan," Bowman began, "I've got some bad news. I need your unit to scramble right away. We've got an incoming capital ship we're about to engage and we'll need some bomber support."

"Okay, we can get out there right away."

"There's more," Bowman said. "I need you to bring a passenger to the surface on an urgent mission."

That's the bad news, Nolan thought. "Um ... are you serious?"

"Unfortunately, I am. You'll be taking Agent Alexander down to the planet and dropping her off so she can rendezvous with the marines."

"But I heard the weather patterns are insane." Nolan pressed a hand against his face before continuing. "Yes, sir. When will she be down here?"

"She's on her way now. Get your ships prepped and launch as soon as possible." Bowman paused again but something in silence suggested he had more to say. When he spoke again, he lowered his voice, just above a whisper. "I'd really appreciate it if you could ensure a smooth and safe deployment of the agent, Nolan."

"Absolutely, sir," Nolan said. "I'll do everything in my power to make it okay."

"Thank you. Bowman out."

Rumors floated around that Bowman and Alexander had a thing together, but he didn't know if was true. Nolan didn't have any sort of pulse on the activities of the officers but that last moment, the little request, spoke of something outside a professional concern. *Consider that chatter confirmed.*

Nolan let the rest of the team know what was coming. He initiated the startup process for his ship then dropped the ramp in the back for Agent Alexander. She'd have to ride in the small hold, which fortunately for her had seats. There were four in total, each practically on top of the other. Four passengers would have to be cozy.

One would probably find it dark and isolated. The cockpit was located up two stairs and obscured from view by the ceiling. She wouldn't have visibility on Nolan and would only have coms to keep her company. There weren't any windows down there either, which was probably for the best considering the weather.

Flight Lieutenant Micah Zane approached, wearing a strange expression. "Hey, what's going on? What's with the ramp?"

"I have a quick side gig to take care of before I can join you guys," Nolan said. "But don't worry, you'll be fine while I'm gone."

"I'm not worried about myself," Micah said. "But going down there ... I mean, Raptor said it was nuts. They had to take to high altitude. There's no way enemy fighters are cruising around down there due to the fierce winds."

"That's good news for me, right?" Nolan grinned. "Means no one's going to be shooting at me."

Micah shook his head. "Sometimes, you're a little insane. You know that, right?"

"Aren't we all?" Nolan saw Agent Alexander enter the hangar. "Sorry, Micah. My passenger is here. You're in charge until I get back."

"See you later, sir." Micah walked away, shaking his head.

Agent Alexander replaced him, standing at the bottom of the ramp. Her dark brown hair was tied back in a tight ponytail and she wore a black tactical suit. A rifle hung from her left shoulder, a pistol rested low on her right leg and she carried a satchel which looked fairly heavy from the way it strained the strap.

"Hello." Nolan stepped down and shook her hand. "I'll be your pilot this afternoon. Welcome aboard Rhino Air." He gestured for her to step aboard. "Today there will be no inflight movie, so I do apologize for that but we do have an excellent seat with no visibility and just enough cushion to make it seem like we've heard about comfort before."

Alexander chuckled. "Thank you. I appreciate you doing this."

"It's my pleasure, Agent Alexander. Sort of."

"Cassie," she said. "Please, you can call me Cassie."

"In that case, you can call me Nolan." He gestured to the safety straps. "You'll want to make sure those are securely fastened before we go and put in an earpiece or you'll be down here all alone in the dark. Believe me, it's way too creepy for that. We had to check it out during our initial flight training with these bad boys and I didn't like it."

"Something tells me this won't be flying the friendly skies," Cassie said.

"From what I understand," Nolan replied, "and no bullshit, we're about to go to the most angry skies either of us has ever seen. But ... this ship's pretty robust. She should make it without too much trouble. Just hang on tight, and trust that I've been doing this for a very long time."

"I will." Cassie secured her equipment then sat down, pulling on the seat belt.

Nolan crawled into the cockpit and lifted the ramp. His ship was powered up and ready to go. Tower clearance came through before he even asked. He lifted off and moved toward the exit. "Hey, tower," he said, grinning, "it's almost like you want to get rid of me or something. I feel like I should be offended."

"Cut the chatter, Rhino One," Warrant Officer Vernon replied. He'd been on tower control since the Gnosis hadn't done more than moved about space near Earth orbit. He held a familiar relationship with all of the pilots on board, which meant they took his gruff disposition in stride.

Nolan watched his scanner, calling out that he cleared the hangar bay force field and was setting course for the surface. *Wish me luck guys,* he thought. Voicing it would only make his passenger nervous. Peering at their destination, his shoulders slumped. The storms were clearly visible from orbit.

That place is like the ninth circle of hell. Nolan shook his head. "Here we go, Agent. Looks like we've got … two minutes to atmosphere and then … I don't know what to expect from that point on. Reports say the weather changes frequently and without warning so let's just hope we catch a window. Otherwise …"

"Yes?" Cassie asked.

"Well, we're going to experience some slight turbulence on our way into Hellweather Airport." Nolan smirked. "Shields will protect us against the lightning, if that becomes a problem, but I'm more worried about these winds. My scans are showing they're near hurricane levels in some parts."

"That's what I understand," Cassie said. "Wait! I can try to plot a safe path down to the facility! Put together a course that cuts around the worst of the storms."

"I'm way ahead of you," Nolan replied, "but thanks for the offer."

"Sorry …" Cassie cleared her throat after the word. He imagined her blushing, which was definitely a pleasing visual. He understood why Commander Bowman took an interest. The woman was beautiful. How she caught planet duty was beyond him but whatever bit of bad luck had sent her down to hang out with the marines drifted Nolan's way too.

They hit atmosphere, cutting through a reasonable window to avoid burn up. The shields lit up in front of him, glowing red and blue. His ship began shaking, subtly at first then more violently the further down he went. Gripping the flight stick with his right hand, he worked the throttle with his left.

"Are we in the storm?" Cassie called out. Now she was scared, he could hear it in the pitch of her voice.

"No, I'm afraid not." Nolan kept his own tone calm even as adrenaline rushed through him. "We're about … thirty seconds from encountering our first natural event. Right now, it looks like it'll be smooth until the surface but this planet might have another idea for us. Okay, I need to concentrate now."

Nolan hit the first set of clouds and an alarm went off, indicating high winds. Rain pounded the vessel, glancing off the shields. Without them, his cockpit would've been covered in beads and streaks. Visibility was terrible, not even five miles out. A particular strong gale struck him from the left, knocking him a good three hundred feet off course.

That's the stuff, right there. Nolan corrected his course, ensuring they were still on the right path. Thunder erupted around them, a great crash that made his ears ring. Something flashed to his left, likely lightning and he instinctually veered away from the blast. *How far down do these clouds go?*

He checked the altimeter and noted they still had twenty-thousand feet to descend. *Apparently, I don't do enough trans-atmospheric flight.* The fact was, he didn't know exactly how the clouds should be. He hadn't flown on Earth for a few years. Another heavy gust brought his thoughts back to the moment, tossing them another few hundred feet to the left.

This is intense. Nolan noticed a tinge in his stomach, some reaction to the sudden motions. He only registered it peripherally, but his passenger might've been losing her lunch in a major way. He wondered if it was the time to let her know they didn't have any barf bags on board … which meant if she did get sick, he would be stuck with it for the rest of the mission.

Oh well. That's how it goes sometimes.

Nolan cut through the clouds and saw the wasteland beneath him. Gray-brown nothingness spread out as far as the eye could see, broken up only by the facility they were heading toward. He altered course to get to the rear, moving swiftly toward the drop off point. It reminded him of a post-apocalyptic movie. The isolation alone gave him the creeps.

And people work down here! Lightning slammed into the roof of the ship, causing another alarm. He checked, noting the shields had fully absorbed the blow. Another bout of thunder hit, then more rain. The ship was battered around far worse, shaking like it was having an absolute fit.

Nolan struggled to steady her, but he couldn't do it. All he could do was control the descent with thrusters. He'd definitely be talking to the shuttle pilots about how they brought their vehicles down without incident. Those things were far less maneuverable than the bomber and Nolan really had to fight.

The altimeter showed he had less than five thousand feet. He tried to slow down but the wind wasn't having any of it. He was being shoved, forced down at an alarming rate. Diverting power to the engines, he kicked on full retro rockets. The ship began to slow but he was pressed hard into his safety harness.

Another lightning blast hit him, this time cutting straight through the shields. Instruments went haywire and his computer shut down. The altimeter was not digital and still allowed him to see they were only eight hundred feet from landing. He pulled the nose up and dropped the landing gear, hitting the ground hard enough to be jostled about.

"Cassie," Nolan shouted into the com. He disengaged his safety harness and headed down into the hold. "Are you okay?"

She looked up at him, face pale with a slight green tinge. She held up a thumb, offering a weak smile. "I didn't throw up ... through some miracle."

"That's something to be proud of." Nolan motioned toward the door. "When you're ready, I'll pop the hatch. I have to conduct some repairs before I can get out of here."

"What happened?"

He explained how diverting power to the engines weakened the shields enough for the lightning to get through. "My systems are wonky so hopefully I can get them back online before I head up to help with the fight. Anyway, that's not your problem. I've got turrets to keep bad guys away. Just go. Do what you've got to do."

"Thank you." Cassie put her backpack on and grabbed her rifle. "I appreciate you doing this."

"Gotta be honest," Nolan said while tapping the button to open the ramp, "I wouldn't have missed it for the world, huh? See you later, Agent. Good luck."

Cassie looked out at the rain and leaned to see where she was going before dashing off.

Nolan closed the ship up, engaged his automated defenses and took a moment to look around his surroundings. "Okay, then. Nothing quite like trying to fix your ship in the middle of a storm on a hostile planet. Good times. Commander

Bowman should be a travel agent when he retires. I'm definitely making that recommendation … if I ever get home."

***

Chapter 6

Anna Jager closed on her target, keeping a wary eye out for the rotating weapons she'd already encountered. She needed less than twenty seconds to be in range. Her shields still hadn't started recharging and she initiated her automated repair systems to check the generator. It was the only logical thing that could be broken but why didn't it show up on a damage report?

She got in range, firing her beam weapons. Both shots struck the enemy just below the engines. The target's shields reacted, brightening and immediately winking out. Anna took that opportunity, firing a missile and blasting away with her mass drivers. Chunks of metal popped off the hull of her opponent and it slowed down, giving the missile a chance to catch up.

The enemy turned into a ball of orange and purple. An ejection pod flew free of the fire. Anna took a deep breath and adjusted her course, heading back toward the fight. A large blip appeared on her scanner, something behind her. She glanced over her shoulder and saw an approaching Kalrawv destroyer, lumbering toward the action.

"I think we're about to get a lot more company," Anna announced. "I've got a destroyer on my six ... plenty far away but it's closing fast."

"Catch back up to us," Preston said. "We've whittled the enemy down here but Jonny's going to have to return to the Gnosis."

"They knocked out my shields," Jonny added. "I've got engine damage and one of my beam weapons won't respond."

Anna shook her head. "Get out of there. Go back to the ship right now. We'll hold the rest. On that topic though, I've got my automated repair looking at the shield generator and it's not coming back with any news. Have the rest of you tried it?"

"I did," Preston replied. "Mine hasn't found the problem yet either."

Bella said, "Pretty sure we're dealing with a relay. Maybe not even fried ... just ... offline."

"I'll be back with you guys in ..." Anna checked her distance. "One minute. How many enemies are still up?"

"One," Preston replied.

"Zero," Simon corrected. "Just got him."

Anna checked the scanner again. The destroyer had yet to deploy additional fighters but it if did, they would need some reinforcements. "Nice work, guys. I'm going to patch into the Gnosis and let them know we'll need some help. Maybe

Raptor can leave their surface patrol. They're just skimming orbit anyway."

"We need to figure out this shield thing," Preston said. "I'm going to take this opportunity to dive into it. Maybe Jonny can figure something out back on the ship. Either way, without understanding that, we're at a huge disadvantage."

"Agreed." An alarm went off in Anna's cockpit and she checked scans again. She had five enemy ships coming in fast. *Where the hell did they come from?* "I've got incoming and they are really screaming! I'm not sure how they snuck up on me."

"Call in Raptor," Preston replied. "They might have a chance of getting to you in time."

"I hope so." Anna put in the call and engaged her afterburners to keep out of firing distance. They were closing fast but she had a head start. With any luck, she'd have some help long before they could start shooting.

That's wishful thinking. A tinge of fear gripped her stomach, but she shoved it aside. There was no time to worry about the incoming attack. She needed to buy time and survive, two of the most difficult objectives she'd faced in a long time.

***

Dennis Arden's Mustang squadron had the opportunity to fly with the Pahxin, backing them up in their operation against the capital ships. After spending time with Dala, he wasn't nearly as enthusiastic about the mission as he might've been. Their view involved victory at all costs where humans squeezed in a desire to survive.

Dala took the lead with nearly thirty Pahxin ships and six from the Gnosis. Once the scanners picked up incoming fighters, she ordered them into action. They weren't quite to their targets when she clicked onto the open tactical net and offered up some observations concerning their opponents.

"My computer suggests these are experimental fighters," Dala said, "a Kalrawv test run. This holds the potential to be good for us in the sense that they may have bugs to work out. Unfortunately, we do not have a clear understanding of how they have armed these things so that will be a dangerous trial and error."

I'll say, Dennis thought. All the alien ships they faced were trial and error for the Gnosis crew. The Pahxin faced dozens of threats throughout their time in space so it became especially terrifying to think that the Pahxin didn't know exactly what to expect. Their experience didn't help, which made the fight all the more frightening.

"I recommend pass by tactics," some random Pahxin spoke over the com. "Draw their fire so we can see what we're up against. I volunteer."

For what? Dennis thought. "What's a pass by tactic?"

"Renka draws their fire," Dala replied, "and we see what happens."

"There has to be a better way than that," Dennis replied. "Surely, we can just … I don't know … rely on scans from the Stalwart?" He checked his own and noted that while his computer came up with a good reading on their shields and propulsion, there was no information at all on the weapons. "How is that possible?"

Dala explained, "They've elected to hide a specific aspect of their ship from scans. I've seen it before but from what I heard, it can be very expensive. Perhaps they've found a way around the cost … or maybe they don't care. Either way, the pass by request is approved. Ensure they know you are a threat or they might not take the bait."

Dennis wanted to protest but he bit his tongue. The Pahxin ship darted away from the formation, flying straight toward the incoming enemy forces. At current speed, the two forces would meet within minutes. One way or another, there would be a major engagement. They'd know what they were facing regardless if they practically sacrificed one of their own.

The Stalwart blasted one of the capital ships as their conflict erupted, obliterating the craft in a matter of moments. Dennis winced when the destroyer exploded, surprised by the firepower leveraged against it. The Gnosis packed a punch, he'd seen them take down ships they probably had no business fighting but nothing went down that quickly for them.

Dennis's attention was brought back to the pass by fighter who charged his opponents and opened up, blasting away at the nearest enemies. They immediately broke formation, putting on a burst to chase him. Flashes popped from their weapons, brief green lights that winked in and out of existence instantly.

"Are those the weapons?" Flight Lieutenant Shane Goring asked. "Are they discharging rounds or beams?"

Dennis checked his scanner. The readings came back, indicating an energy weapon of some sort. "They aren't using projectiles. High concentration, short range beams."

Dala added, "They seem to lock target and specifically fire according to that range. The weakness I see is the need to lock on. They likely cannot blind fire those in an effort to hit. If they can, the range would be even more limited."

The pilot flying around out there maneuvered like a demon, avoiding his opponents with incredible grace and skill. It still horrified Dennis to think they were using him as bait, to get an idea of what they were up against. "Now that we know, permission to engage and help that pilot?"

"Granted," Dala said. "Hold on, Renka. We're coming to your aid."

"Hold fast," Renka replied. "I've been hit and have more data for you. When these blasts hit shields, they seem to affect the generator's ability to recharge. I'm at seventy-percent and it has not increased. Keep that in mind as you go into this brawl. They have a distinct advantage."

"They could nickel and dime us," Shane said. "Any way to reinforce the generator?"

"Not while in flight," Dennis said. "Okay, so … do what you would've done anyway and avoid being hit. Let's go." He jammed his throttle forward, kicking on the afterburners. The rest of Mustang kept pace with him and the Pahxin around them did the same. They plunged toward their targets, each firing as they went.

Dennis maneuvered to avoid colliding with his target, dove under the next and banked hard to the right in a final effort to survive their flyby. He noted his shields miraculously remained fully charged. Spinning around, he maneuvered to engage his first target, noting they lost two Pahxin ships in that exchange.

Shane reported his shields were already down to fifty percent. The rest of Mustang made it through okay.

Time to see how good their defenses are. Dennis noted one of the enemies closing on an ally's tail. He swept over and acquired a solid firing solution, blasting away with his beam weapons. The enemy veered off but Dennis stayed on him, firing again. He clipped his shields, knocking them out.

The enemy's wings looked odd and as he leaned forward, he saw the weapons rotating. *What, are you kidding me?* He fired again just as the guns began to aim, this time tearing through the ship's engines. It tumbled forward, spinning wildly before exploding. Dennis veered to the side.

"They can redirect their weapons," Dennis announced. "Be cautious with that." He craned his neck to see if Renka made it, but he couldn't see him and his scanner didn't differentiate individual Pahxin ships. They had lost five in total, but the enemy was taking a beating. They were down twelve ships.

"Splash three for me," Alicia Quinn announced. Hot off her promotion, it didn't temper her wild flying techniques. She came up on Dennis's wing, forming up. "We've got three incoming on this position. I say we take them head on, weapons hot and see who flinches first. You with me?"

"No," Dennis replied. "Not with those weapons. Let's climb and come down on top of them. You take their three o'clock, I'll go for nine and we'll flank them."

"Not as much fun but you're the boss." Alicia veered off, performing a barrel roll as she moved into position. He found his own and they counted down before diving. The enemy seemed intent on attacking a specific ship but as soon as

the two Earth ships began firing at them, they tried to break off.
"No you don't."

Alicia plunged below the ship and flipped around, a stunning and tight maneuver that had to have rattled her bones. She came at her target, blasting away at his underside. The shields went down just as she flew by and Dennis thought to support her but she spun in place, dropping a missile then jamming the afterburners forward when she finished the revolution.

As she flew off, her opponent exploded.

Dennis fired away at his own target, missing due to incredible evasion. He tried to anticipate the motions but couldn't lead him. Finally, he launched a missile and fired to his target's left. That did the trick and he scored a hit, but the shields absorbed it. The missile came close to connecting when the thrust suddenly stopped and it simply began to drift.

"It just did something to my missile!"

An alarm went off and the cockpit lit up, flashing with warnings across the scanning screen. He took several blasts to his tail before he spun to the left and dove. Shields showed at forty-percent. The enemy who caught up to him flew off, leaving him alone for a moment. No other damage presented itself, but it happened insanely fast.

Those guns they have are incredible!

"I'm getting a message from the Stalwart," Dala said. "There are bombers incoming. Mustang One and Five, you're with me. We should be able to handle them. The rest of you mop up this rabble. I want space superiority by the time I get back."

She requested Dennis and Alicia to join her, which didn't surprise Dennis at all. Dala expressed how impressed she was with both of them on several occasions. Considering they were about to go up against some vessels that should've been in better armor, it would be a challenge to take them down with only three fighters.

"You sure we don't need more help?" Dennis asked.

"I could do it alone," Alicia replied. "If you guys want to hang back here."

"I appreciate your enthusiasm," Dala said, "but we do this together. Don't worry. I'll get you back to gaining glory for your people quickly enough. For now, form on me and prepare to take these out. I don't want them taking any shots at the Stalwart while they're busy."

Dennis fell in and matched her speed. Their targets were two minutes out. Plenty of time to catch his breath and discover exactly what was wrong with his generator. If he could discover the problem, he could eliminate the enemy's advantage completely, but chances were good he had to survive the rest of the battle on compromised shields.

Never a dull moment serving on the Gnosis. Dennis dialed in his computer and started the internal diagnostic.

***

Gizan watched his scan, waiting for it to locate any trace of the Trindisha hiding somewhere on the planet. He refused to believe Kalrawv had no idea what they were sitting on. While the resources on the world were extensive and certainly worth exploiting, they seemed like a fantastic cover for a much larger prize.

He focused his search on their mining operations first. Overhead, a battle began between the Kalrawv security forces and the military. Multiple ships came down to the surface, shuttles carrying soldiers intent on taking the base he assumed. When Gizan sent his own signal to the Tol'An, he made sure they sent ground troops as well.

Battle might've been inevitable depending on how well the security forces did their jobs. Their weapons certainly were terrifying enough to do some serious damage. Even in that ridiculous power armor, those human soldiers would not survive a tangle with sonic weaponry. After Gizan saw what it did to Dak, he knew how frightening Kalrawv tech had become.

However, he didn't feel entirely confident in them. The humans swept through his own forces and took his hostages right out from under him. That took more than just daring and nerve. They had skill and if the Kalrawv underestimated them, they would likely fail and probably lose the base in short order.

The door opened and two officers charged in. They nearly tripped over the bodies and Gizan directed his weapon at them, firing twice. Each of them screamed half a second before the blasts connected with their torsos, disrupting their internal organs and sending them to the ground, convulsing as they died.

He checked the scanner, feeling impatient with the time it was taking. People were coming to the control room to direct the battle, to try sending messages for help and to organize their people. More would arrive soon, and he wouldn't be able to kill them all. Not if they showed up en masse with soldiers.

None of their stored searches indicated they knew how to hunt for Trindisha energy. If they did have any clue, they were hiding it behind routine checks for different types of ore and atmospheric anomalies. Footsteps in the hallway dragged his attention away from the screen. He counted at least four incoming.

Gizan moved to the side of the door, pressing himself against the wall. Three men burst in with weapons, again nearly tripping on the bodies directly in front of them. The distraction provided an opportunity.

Gizan shot the first one in the back of the head. The victim didn't even scream. A sickening crunch sounded as the body collapsed to the ground. He redirected the weapon, pulling the trigger again but it merely clicked. His eyes widened. The other two men turned on him and he threw himself forward, ramming into them before they could shoot.

They tumbled to the floor, flailing their arms and hammer Gizan as he came down on top of him. He attempted to block some of the blows, but they scored several shots to the face and chest.

Retaliating, he took a blow to the nose in exchange to jam his thumb into his victim's throat. The man's mouth opened wide and he began gasping, grasping at his neck. The other grabbed Gizan by the arm and tried to drag him to the ground. They began to wrestle, vying for control of the conflict.

Gizan came out on the bottom. He wrapped his knees around the man's sides and squeezed, fending off his assailant's hands from getting a grip on his throat. They strained, each grunting through the conflict before the pressure against the man's soft bits became too much.

His struggle lessened and he cried out. Gizan twisted one of his wrists, snapping it in a quick gesture. The man stumbled away and Gizan grabbed the other man's firearm. Rolling onto his back he shot the man three times in the torso, sending him cascading backward, obliterating his bones and internal organs.

Gizan rose, checking the scanner screen. A possibility presented itself, a hint of a specific type of power in one of the deeper mine shafts. He needed to get moving if he wanted to be there in a reasonable amount of time. The trip would take a minimum of twenty minutes and that was if he didn't have to fight anyone else.

Of course, the uniform might get him pretty far and Kalrawv had the marines to worry about. He wiped his search and headed out, rushing through the opposite door as more soldiers arrived. The woman might recover, she may even reveal his description to security, but it wouldn't matter.

By the time they knew he was running around their facility, it would be too late to stop him. His companions would arrive and he'd have the Trindisha. Kalrawv already lost the fight. They were simply going through the death throes before realizing it.

***

Heat figured the Kalrawv security forces would dig in near the central hub. That would be the largest fight in their effort to find the Orb. Afterward, he doubted they would be able to mount a real solid defense again, especially not after losing so many. He based his assessment on the idea of victory for his side.

"We're on your six!" Gillet shouted. "I have visual now!"

"Good," Heat grumbled. "It's about time. Prepare to move out."

"Heat?" Cassie's voice crackled over their com. "Do you read me?"

"I do," Heat replied. "What's up? I don't have much time to talk. We're about to storm the central building."

"I'm here," Cassie said. "I'm just inside near a wall that got blown to hell. Where are you?"

Heat sighed. "You have got to be kidding. You came down here? Why? I thought we had a plan."

"It wasn't working," Cassie explained. "The interference from the weather and God knows what else prevented me from scanning the planet. I couldn't tell you where to find the Orb but now that I'm here, I'll use their equipment to locate it."

"How'd you even get here?"

"Nolan gave me a ride," Cassie said. "His bomber made it but he's having to conduct some repairs out there right now. We were struck by lightning just before touchdown. You wouldn't believe how intense *that* was."

"I ..." Heat bit his tongue before replying. "Got it. You're back where Gillet and his guys just were. Follow the hallway to catch up to us but you probably want to hang back. They're using sonic weapons and to say they're nasty is a dramatic understatement. People are obliterated by these things."

"Ooph. Got it. I'll be there soon."

Heat turned to Gillet and shook his head. "She'll hang back and we cleared that section so we advance now. Come on, guys."

Heat led the way, approaching another sealed door. This one was not locked so the marines stacked up on either side for cover and prepared to breach. He spoke softly, counting them down before he'd open it up. Their HUDs would attempt to scan for weapons, but the central hub was the largest part of the structure.

If there were any civilians, they would be in there. What was worse, the Kalrawv security guys weren't wearing uniforms easy to distinguish from regular attire. Tarnished black coats, tan cargo pants and various kinds of boots. Definitely not military style. As Heat expected, targeting would be a nightmare.

Heat opened the door and before any of them even moved, a couple of sonic blasts wheezed past them, splashing into the ceiling. *Theory proven. Damn it.* He and Gillet popped a couple of flash bang grenades, something to disorient the crew inside. So far, none of them wore protective gear so they should've been plenty effective.

The grenades cracked, drawing out a couple strangled cries. Heat and Gillet led the way with the other marines spilling in after them. They found cover as Erskin opened up, blasting away with a fully automatic spray from his rifle. Heat couldn't imagine he'd already seen a target, but he didn't have time to confirm.

They entered a chamber with a fifteen-foot ceiling and kiosks on the left and right. Doors led to other long hallways stretching to different wings. Consoles and benches, plants and statues blocked line of sight through the area. Kalrawv forces hid amongst these bits of cover and as the violence erupted, many people ran for the doors.

"Contact!" Vine yelled. "Er ... everywhere!"

"Check your targets," Heat said. "Make sure you know who you're shooting before you pull the trigger." He leaned out to the right of his cover, a massive computer panel that controlled some kind of vending machine. A Kalrawv man held a civilian tightly, using him as a human shield. He faced to the right, giving Heat a small window to get him.

Heat took aim, zeroing in on his target's head. The man fired a couple of times, seemingly blind to suppress whoever he thought he saw. Heat pulled the trigger once, nailing his opponent right below the ear. The bullet exited out the other side, creating a rust colored mist before the body collapsed.

The civilian screamed and ran for the door in blind panic, exiting as he reached it.

That one shot seemed to ignite a wild fire fight. Sonic blasts filled the air. The overlapping wheezing of the weapons sounded like an entire fraternity attempting to force themselves to vomit. Rifle shots responded, each crack echoing off the walls. Heat's HUD showed at least fifteen opponents, though some of them still could've been civilians.

Heat's cover console was struck several times, but the metal seemed to defy damage from the attack. He crouched and moved to the opposite site, glancing out to see a couple of men using a flipped over kiosk as cover. They had to bend low in order to be obscured and neither of them bothered to hide themselves.

The metal around them sparked with missed bullets, slapping the ground and bouncing harmlessly away. Heat took aim and prepared to shoot again when a sonic blast slapped into his rifle, knocking it aside just as he pulled the trigger. His shots went wide and his weapon vibrated against his cover, nearly shaking it out of his hand.

Heat's HUD showed severe damage to the weapon, bad enough that it recommended he not fire it again. Letting it hang from the sling, he drew his pistol and looked for the guy who shot at him. Another blast nearly took his face off so he withdrew back to the safety of cover, cursing loudly.

"You get hit?" Gillet asked.

"My weapon did."

Private Taras let out a gurgling scream. Heat's HUD indicated his life signs had dropped. More cries filled the air, Kalrawv security forces being taken out. Heat risked another glance and this time saw his opponent, a guy hiding in a shop to the left. Just as Heat peeked out, the man fired at him again, this time going high.

Okay, bastard. Heat quickly fired his pistol, unleashing half the magazine at the shop. His target tried to fall back but at least one round caught his shoulder. Blood splattered the wall behind him and he remained hidden.

Two Kalrawv security personnel charged their position, shouting as they did. They got off a good four shots before they were annihilated by rifles from three different positions. As they dropped to the ground, Heat's target made a run for the door. Heat led him, taking only three shots before he got him in the head.

"How many are left?" Gillet called out. "Anyone got a good number?"

"Two," Cassie said. "I'm reading two armed people still alive but they're moving pretty slow. They might be injured."

"Be cautious," Heat said. "Bosh, take a look."

"Yes, sir." Bosh didn't sound thrilled but he stepped out into the area, moving slowly. "I hope you guys remember what providing cover means."

"Letting you get shot," Brock said. "Just find the last targets, man."

Heat shook his head, leaning out to take a look. He couldn't imagine they got them all. Some must've fled with the civilians, probably to find some reinforcements. The marines found themselves in a sort of general gathering area. Stairs and elevators went up to different sections of the base.

Living quarters made up some of the hallways though there were also more important systems in them such as facilities, generators and basic environmental controls. Each of them would be fantastic places for people to hide but as far as Heat was concerned, they could stay there.

Providing they locked down whatever area Cassie needed to locate their prize, they'd be good to go.

"I found them," Bosh said. "They're done. Someone got these guys good."

"Disarm them then," Heat replied. "Establish a perimeter. I want this place locked down while we figure out where we're going next. Agent Alexander, can any of this stuff help you with what you need to do? There are definitely some computers in here. Mostly shops and a couple vending machines."

"Maybe." Cassie entered the room and stepped up to Heat. In his power armor, he towered over her by a good four feet. She scanned the area and gestured to a room near the opposite exit. "I'm going to try over there. Do you think it's safe?"

"I'll check it." Heat headed over there, peering inside. A woman held her hands up, closing her eyes tightly. She was unarmed, probably in her late fifties, and so terrified, she couldn't stop trembling. "Just a civilian here. Vine, I want this woman secured. Let's lock her up in the office over there with any others you find."

"I'm on it, Gunny." Vine came over and spoke through his external speaker. "Ma'am, we're not going to hurt you. Please come this way so we can secure you somewhere safe." He had to help her stand and led her away. She started crying halfway across the room, really sobbing the whole way.

Must've seen some of the bodies. Heat shook his head. *This is messed up.* "Come on, Cassie. It's ready."

"Thanks." Cassie hurried into the room, putting her tablet on the table. She tapped away, staring at the screen beside it. "Yes, this is patched into the central network. It probably doesn't have the permissions to get through to what we need to complete the mission, but I can establish a better connection to the ship from here."

"Yeah?" Heat nodded. "That's better than nothing."

"If I do that, it might mean we can use our own scanners ... but I'm not getting my hopes up. I still feel like we're going to have to take their control room."

"It's never easy," Heat muttered.

"Gnosis, this is Agent Alexander." Cassie tapped on her tablet for a few moments. "Do you read? Please respond."

Fielding's voice piped through Heat's helmet. "Can you hear me, Gunny? Agent Alexander? Hello?"

"I hear you," Heat said. "We've got a boost!"

"Great!" Fielding sounded relieved. "Give me a sitrep. What's going on down there? Have you located the Orb?"

"We're progressing," Heat replied, "but we're not there yet. I'll give you the quick version ... We've still got a lot of ground to cover."

Chapter 7

Ulian received a report stating the Gnosis was about to engage a destroyer. He clenched his fist. How did the Kalrawv Group manage to hide an entire capital ship from their sensor sweep? *It has to be the interference in this system. The weather or maybe they've come up with some technical way to do it.*

Regardless, the interruption to the operation annoyed him.

Ulian turned to Morala. "The Gnosis is under attack by a destroyer."

"What?" Morala immediately turned to her screen, staring at the scan. "How did those bastards ... And we have our own problems." The ship shook from a massive barrage as their opponents opened up on them. Erda initiated more evasive maneuvers, jostling them in their seats. "Viran, contact the Gnosis and see if they require aid."

"I'm afraid we're in no position to provide it," Ulian said. "Unless they maneuver toward us that is. Then perhaps ..." He hummed. "We have the remaining destroyers, the bombers and that battleship that's remaining out of range, waiting to have us whittled down before engaging."

"They'll run," Morala replied. "I can almost guarantee it. They have no desire to push us and they want to play the victim. They can't do that if they are dead."

Ulian tilted his head. "Look at the tactics. Exhaust our fighters, challenge them with bombers, hit us with the destroyers … They're not running right now and they could while we're busy. No, they believe they can win this fight or they wouldn't be sticking around. However, they're playing a dangerous game. Even if we lose, they will be vulnerable."

Viran spoke up, "Commander, the Gnosis states they have their situation under control. I am also picking up a spatial anomaly consistent with hyperspace. It appears Kalrawv may have been able to call for reinforcements after all."

"Impossible!" Morala shook her head. "We jammed them the moment we arrived."

"I agree." Ulian spoke more cautiously about it. "I have a bad feeling this is a third party."

"The Tol'An?" Morala asked.

Ulian shrugged. "There aren't many others who would want in on this action. It's disturbing though. How would they have known to come here at all? Unless they discovered how to get the information out of their Orbs." He stared at the floor in thought until the tremble of the ship brought him back to the moment. "Doesn't matter now how they know."

"Quite right." Morala turned to Erda. "Have you targeted the next destroyer?"

"Yes, ma'am. I'm doing a dance over here." Erda paused. "A second volley is on the way. They survived my first pass with some good evasive maneuvers. I don't think they'll make it this time."

The weapons discharged, blasting through the enemy shields and obliterating the hull. In the same moment, the other five destroyers unleashed another attack. Erda hit his panel hard and the ship lurched downward, crushing everyone into their seats with the sudden motion. Ulian winced and remained tensed in anticipation of a blow that never came.

"Full evasion!" Erda clapped his hands once before tapping his screen with swift fingers. "Those bombers are still closing. How're the fighters doing with closing in on them?"

Morala got on the com personally and sent a message, informing the pilots they needed to make haste. Ulian watched the screen, noting the telltale bright flashes of ships arriving from hyperspace. There were ten of them, each without any identifying marks but he already recognized their silhouettes.

They were certainly Tol'An and half of them rushed the planet.

"We need to send reinforcements to the ground units," Ulian said. "I'll organize it." He got on the com and sent a message to have soldiers assemble for immediate departure.

They would have a rough trip considering how many fighters were already roaming around and the addition of Tol'An hostiles complicated it further.

"This is getting ridiculous," Morala muttered. "We should've brought a fleet."

"This was supposed to be subtle," Ulian said. "A surgical strike at a faraway place. We've still got this. Remain focused. Kalrawv is about to be hit from both sides. If we're lucky, Tol'An will deal with the battleship. After that ... well ... you know how the terrorist commanders are. Zealous ... but terrible."

"I guess it is the lesser of two evils," Morala replied. "Hit them again, Erda. Don't let up. Viran, let the Gnosis know we're sending their marines some help and if they haven't already seen it, tell them about our guests. It appears likely they'll have to face them on the ground. We can't intercept those vessels driving straight for the planet."

Ulian leaned back in his chair, considering the situation. The extra forces made the situation more dangerous but at the same time, it worked to their advantage in space. Distracting Kalrawv meant they had a better chance of avoiding those projectiles that could practically ignore shields.

He never thought he'd consider the Tol'An to be worth much but at least this time, they proved to have some minor value.

***

Alicia Quinn absolutely loved flying and found her role as a combat pilot to be the pinnacle of testing her skills. The promotion she received didn't mean nearly as much as the continued right to sit behind the controls of a fighter, pushing herself toward her absolute limits.

The Kalrawv Group weapons made the current conflict all the more exhilarating. Avoiding them practically required prescience but she'd only been clipped so far. Their pilots couldn't keep up with her style of rapid, wild maneuvers. Spinning, rolling and sudden banks meant they had a hard time getting a lock on her.

By all rights, she should've stayed with the rest of the force and continued the brawl.

Attacking the bombers wouldn't be particularly hard. They likely employed turrets for defense and would continue their courses regardless of what was thrown at them. Their armor alone meant they should be able to take a few hits, even from missiles but there were only four of them.

The Gnosis would've sent an entire squadron against them, six ships to take them down. Dala seemed to think three would do the trick. Alicia didn't necessarily disagree, but would they be able to take them out before the bombers deployed ordnance against the Stalwart? That was another story.

"We're nearly in range," Dala said. "Prepare yourselves."

Dennis grunted. "My scans aren't showing their weapons either."

"Same trick as the fighters," Dala replied. "Though the silhouette suggests blasters akin to what we've seen from their destroyers. They'll pack a mean punch that might go straight through shields. You'll want to avoid them at all costs. Also, I'm reading the weak points are not the engines like normal. It's the nose and the top."

"Convenient," Alicia said. "They have emitters between the two thrusters in the back. That's to keep their engines safe from a rear assault. Okay, so we go from the top. That's cool with me. Permission to break formation and attack?"

Dala clicked her tongue before answering. "Hold tight. I think they have range on us."

Green blasts erupted from the turrets, hurtling toward them rapidly. They missed without requiring evasive maneuvers but all four of them turned the attacks on them, sending out a screen of energy blasts. Dala led them in a climb, effectively testing the rotation of the cannons and whether they could follow them in three hundred and sixty degrees.

They screamed over the bombers, moving at near to top speed. The blasts continued to follow them until they were long past their targets.

"This'll be interesting." Dala chuckled. "I hope you're ready for some real fancy flying. When you attack, you'll want to maneuver like you never have before. Hit them with everything you've got on your way by. We'll concentrate efforts on the second to the middle. I've marked it on the scanner. If he goes up, he may cause damage to the others."

"Great idea," Dennis said. "But this might be suicide, you realize that, right?"

"We have to stop them from reaching the Stalwart," Dala replied. "I'm not sure what else we have to concern ourselves with."

Alicia figured Dennis was fuming in his cockpit with that answer. He put a lot of stock in risk management, in flying defensively. She personally felt there was a middle ground between his style of flying and Dala's *guts and glory* approach. Fly hard *and* survive. Yes, the line might've been fine, but Alicia had been doing it since their first engagement.

And I'm still fine. Whoa! Alicia flipped and climbed, narrowly avoiding a curtain of blaster fire. She jammed the throttle forward, careening under the bombers while risking the second set of turrets. They opened up, chasing her as she went. As she cleared them, she climbed again, spinning in place.

The maneuver rattled her bones, tossing her about but she managed to maintain her composure, letting her beam weapons fly as well as two missiles. It wasn't exactly the plan Dala had but at least one of the bombers would take some punishment.

Thrusters helped her slow the circle and she rocketed off away from additional attacks.

Scans indicated she'd scored several direct hits on one of the targets, tearing through their shields on the left side. Unfortunately, it wasn't the one Dala and Dennis initiated a coordinated attack on. They strafed the one on the middle right, battering the roof as several turrets chased them on their way by.

Alicia looped around to follow up, dropping another missile at the one she hit a moment ago while planning her own attack run on their communal target. The turrets were facing the wrong way to catch her, and she made a pass without having to dodge at all. This afforded her the luxury of aiming, tearing through the top of the ship before banking away from them.

"The turrets are confused," Dala called out. "They're relying on automation to defend them. Break formation. We'll hit them from multiple angles and continue to provide an ever-changing threat identifier for their AI. Go."

Alicia timed it, letting Dennis take the first run. She kept out of the range of the turrets, counting silently in her head for the chance to make the next attack. Dennis swept in from the rear, blasting away, cutting through the shields. The turrets swung around, the first two shots catching him as he veered off.

His shields didn't even flare up. The back stabilizer came loose, tumbling away. Alicia didn't have time to ask if he was okay. She initiated her own attack run, coming in from the enemy's starboard side. Blasting away with mass drivers. Holes appeared in the hull of her target, tearing straight through and bursting out the other side.

Fire erupted from the holes, globes of orange and purple. Dala followed up, laying into it right behind Alicia. The turrets spun around twice, twitching but no longer shooting. This didn't stop their buddies on the left and right and Alicia narrowly avoided three shots that seemed to skim the bottom of her hull.

No damage registered but she knew she'd come out lucky.

The bomber exploded suddenly, cascading pieces in all directions. They blasted the bombers closest to them, forcing them to veer away and break formation. Alicia's first target darted off back toward his allies while the other two took a loop in an effort to get on course.

Dala flew past Alicia, nearly clipping her she was so close. Alicia spun around and followed, dropping down low enough for a good line of sight on their combined target. They raced toward the one she initially damaged and lit him up, beam weapons nipping at his tail, shredding his shields.

He tried to evade, moving erratically to the left and right but he couldn't outmaneuver the smaller ships. Alicia fired her mass drivers, biting into the enemy's thrusters. Balls of fire exploded from the damage and Dala veered hard to the right. Alicia went the opposite direction just as the second bomber went up.

"I'm on the last two," Dennis shouted. "They're really pushing for the Stalwart!"

Alicia and Dala were a good twenty seconds away. They flew neck and neck to catch up as Dennis made a pass, dropping multiple missiles and beam weapons in the pass. The stabilizer he lost must not have given him too much trouble but as he passed them by, he took another set of shots to his underside.

"Mayday!" Dennis called. "I just lost weapons ... Controls are sluggish ... I think my left thrusters are out."

One of the bombers broke formation to follow Dennis, thrusters pumping out additional fuel to catch up. Alicia narrowed her eyes and focused, firing her weapons even though she was quite a ways off. The attack missed. "Punch out!" She called. "Do it! That guy's all over your ass!"

"I'm working on it! I can't ..." Dennis's com went dead as the shuttle struck him again, knocking his engines out. The pod burst free half a second before the rest of the ship went up and winked out of existence.

"God damn it!" Alicia wrenched her throttle back and slowed down, using her side thrusters to compel her to the left. She caressed the controls, moving in a circle around the bomber to bombard it continually with energy beams.

Turrets swung in her direction, but they couldn't quite lead her. She made a full revolution before dropping two missiles and darting off. The ordnance hammered her target, knocking it to the side. Lights on the hull flickered and winked out and it began to drift. No one ejected but the ship seemed to go dead.

"One left," Alicia muttered.

"I've got it," Dala replied. She cruised up to the side of the bomber and let her weapons fly, slicing through the hull. After being caught up in the destruction of its ally, its defenses were gone.

It turned to run, flying back toward the Kalrawv ships but Dala looped around and blasted him again, blowing it away.

"That's that." Dala formed up with Alicia. "We'll get search and rescue for Arden. Now, I'm getting a message that the Tol'An have shown up."

"Great," Alicia replied in a clipped tone. "That's lovely. I guess we should get back at it then, huh?"

"There are many more ships to take care of." Dala sighed. "Dennis will be fine. Follow my lead and we'll get back to the others. We've done good work so far. We'll wrap it up with a victory shortly enough."

Pretty high cost, Alicia thought. *For both sides.*

***

Desmond stood, watching the view screen as they closed in on the enemy destroyer. They'd be in the thick of it soon enough. Charger squadron already called in Raptor to help fend off the enemy fighters. If they could take out the destroyer quickly, they'd likely remove the last vestige of defense from the Kalrawv roster.

"Tol'An forces have arrived in the system." Salina's announcement made Desmond close his eyes. "They are rapidly approaching the planet … the Stalwart is deploying support to our troops on the surface."

"Do we have to worry about the capital ships?" Desmond asked.

"It's possible we might have two to contend with after they drop their people off," Salina said. "Scans indicate they're moving swiftly but won't be here for some time. Their ETA is five minutes."

"Support for the troops?" Vincent asked.

"Six and a half."

Desmond shook his head. "And those shuttles have to contend with enemy fighters too. This is getting to be a bigger mess than we anticipated." He turned to Salina. "Let Fielding know what's going on with the Tol'An. Vincent, tell the pilots we've got more company. Zach, are the weapons ready?"

"We're hot and ready to go," Zach said. "Give me the word and I'll lay into them as soon as they're in range."

"Fire at will," Desmond said. "I want you to go for first strike. We need to seize the initiative and really put it to them. God knows our people might have the Orb at any moment and will need an extraction. We can't be playing with this bastard while that happens. A lucky shot could end the whole reason we came out here."

"I'm targeting what should be weak points in their vessel, but we don't have this silhouette in the database from the Pahxin." Zach shrugged. "I'm just hoping what I consider logical turns out to be true."

"I trust you." Desmond returned to his seat and looked over the various reports. The marines didn't have much to say but Cassie had linked up with them. He showed that to Vincent who looked somewhat relieved. Nolan was temporarily stuck on the surface while he conducted some field repairs. This left Rhino down one unit.

We won't need them all providing we can take down their shields for the bombs. Desmond considered their opponent for another moment. They still had a good thirty seconds before firing and it looked so painfully peaceful in space directly ahead of them. Off a ways, the Stalwart engaged in a brutal fight but just over the surface of the planet, it felt almost serene.

We'll fix that in just a moment.

The Kalrawv commanders were not to be trifled with. They knew how to fight and how to take advantage of their technology. The next few minutes would be like battling a totally unknown entity. Desmond prepared himself mentally to adjust their tactics, but he couldn't think ahead three moves without knowing the possibilities.

Even with the messages from the Stalwart, he could only guess what they were facing. This particular destroyer didn't look like the ones fighting their allies. It was something else. That meant the concussion beams may or may not be a problem. Desmond erred on the side of assuming that's what they were facing.

If not, it doesn't matter anyway. I'll be fretting over something I can't change.

"Opening fire!" Zach called, tapping his console. The ship whined as the weapons discharged, sending their blasts out in a tight pattern. The destroyer didn't even attempt to evade, didn't move to dodge. The energy from their assault battered their shields like a wrecking ball.

"Minimal shield damage," Salina called. "It appears they have a powerful generator emitting that field. It *might* be one of the only things they can do with that ship. Considering the power output, I wouldn't be surprised if they could not retaliate in any meaningful way."

"Don't put it past them," Vincent said. "For all we know, the ship is probably a flying generator with minimal crew. I'm having the bombers get into position so they can strike on our command."

"Good." Desmond sat down and gripped his chair. "They're counterattacking."

"I'm evading!" Zach got them moving just as a single beam erupted from the enemy ship. It struck the Gnosis, remaining connected for a good five seconds before disappearing. "What the hell was that thing?"

"Some kind of pulse laser," Salina said. "It dropped our forward shields by thirty percent by blasting energy waves the entire time it was in connection. Once it looked on to us, I don't think we could've shaken it off. Perhaps if we go backward next time and force them to extend it? That might even cause them some trouble."

"Good idea." Desmond gestured to Zach. "Keep that in mind and get us firing again. Let me know when the bombers are in position. I want to harass this bastard so he doesn't get too many chances to pull that off. This needs to end quickly, we can't play games considering everything that's at stake."

***

Nolan scanned various parts of the ship, trying to find the section most damaged by the lightning strike. He tried to be methodical, keeping his motions slow to ensure he focused on every part of the vessel, but he had a hard time remaining calm. The storm raged outside again and winds battered the hull, making the bomber rock.

This thing isn't exactly light. The thought made him wonder about the trains that conveyed miners to their work environment. How long did it take them to get used to the weather? Did they ever? Did the Kalrawv Group warn potential employees what they were getting into? Nolan doubted it.

He reached the end of the ship, turned and started up the cargo bay. The internal computer failed to locate the problem, insisting that all systems checked out normal, despite every instrument flickering wildly. A relay must've been trashed, causing a disconnect in the diagnostic system.

But his hand scanner failed to find the problem, even on the second pass. *I have to go outside*. The thought filled him with dread. Wind howled outside and the rain clattered on the hull so hard, he wondered if it might be hail. Even with his helmet on, he didn't know how safe it would be. Especially if the lightning kicked up again.

Nolan returned to the cockpit and scanned the entire area again, desperation driving him to a triple check. Finally, an anomaly came back. His heart leapt and he felt a sense of relief … until it suggested one of the relays near the surface of the hull on the top could be the culprit.

Do I even have what I need to fix that? Nolan considered his resources. If it required a replacement, he would be out of luck but if he simply needed to bypass it, that might be enough. There were two problems. One involved the weather but there were hostile forces out there as well.

He doubted they'd be running around the surface, but he put them down near enough to the facility that anything was possible. Clicking on the com, he tried to raise Cassandra. An indicator on his tablet rotated with one word throbbing slowly: connecting. *Take your time,* he thought. *I've got plenty … not at all*.

"Hello?" Cassie answered. "Who is this?"

"Hey! This is Nolan. I needed to ask you if you guys cleared that wing you entered through. Are there any more hostiles in that section?"

"Not that I'm aware of," Cassie replied. "Why? What's going on?"

"I have to go out on the hull of the bomber and fix something. I'm already going to be dodging lightning, I didn't want to have to dodge gunfire too."

"You should be fine. They're focused on us I believe."

"I'm sorry for you ... but that's good news for me." Nolan frowned. "Sort of. Okay, thanks for the update. Nolan out."

He put his helmet on and secured his mask. Dropping the ramp half way made the roar of the storm all that much wilder. He looked out at the cascading water drifting over the landscape, slapping the ground hard enough to bring dirt up with each gust. *Jesus Christ ...* Nolan moved to the edge and waited, hoping it would slow down.

As expected, it did calm but he had no idea how long it would be before it went wild again. Stepping down the ramp, he was able to reach the roof and he pulled himself up on the slick surface, remaining low. He didn't have to search for the panel in question. It was scorched black and roughly half way along the ship.

He crawled to it, praying silently that the wind wouldn't sweep him off the ship. There was nothing really to hold on to where he was going, no safety per se. The rain made it difficult enough, but any heavy gale would easily sweep him away.

When he reached the panel, he popped it off and found the smoking relay. It would need to be replaced but he thought he might be able to bypass it, giving him a chance to return to orbit. *All I have to do is leave the surface. Once I'm in space, I can struggle bus my way back to the Gnosis and get some repairs.*

The screen on his tablet collected beads of water, making it difficult to read. Nolan found the schematic he needed and reached in to perform a manual adjustment. The switches were tiny, and he had to remove his gloves. *This is probably a bad idea.* He hoped there wasn't some residual power that could shock the hell out of him, but he had to take the chance.

Reaching into the hole, he found the first one easily enough and flipped it. The tablet showed that it worked. The second one, he had to root around for. Just when he thought he'd found it, a sound to his left caught his attention. Ships, descending on the compound, streaked across the sky.

They were heading for the opposite side of the base from him but didn't look like any of the silhouettes he studied in the briefing. *Those aren't Kalrawv or Pahxin.* Nolan swallowed hard. *Oh God. Could those be ... Tol'An? But how? Why? Do we still have a traitor feeding them intelligence?*

Nolan returned his attention to the switch. He needed to hurry so he could warn Cassie and the marines. Hovering over the panel, he used his body to keep as much water out of the panel as possible, but it wasn't working. After a few moments, his fingers were submerged and he still hadn't found the switch.

A heavy wind slapped him from behind, causing his stomach to do a flip. Fortunately, it was just a gentle nudge but it was a promise of what *could* happen. Another set of ships descended on the planet. Nolan remained focused, muttering curses under his breath until he gasped.

Deep in the back right, he found the switch. He pinched it between his index finger and middle finger, jamming it to the side. It made an audible click loud enough to be heard over the weather and through his helmet. For half a second, he thought he might've broken it off but checking the tablet, he found that it was engaged.

Thank God! Nolan jammed the panel into place and pressed it down until it clicked. Shields might hold it in place long enough to get back to the Gnosis but without them, it would probably be gone the moment he took off. Crawling back swiftly, he slipped several times.

Just as he reached aft, he saw a massive cloud of water rushing toward him. Throwing his arms around the left tail wing and braced his feet against the other. The wind slammed the ship so hard, it tilted up before crashing down on the landing gear. The blow nearly dislodged him and he clung tightly, eyes closed.

He had no idea how long it lasted but when it finally subsided, he guessed it had only been a few moments, twenty seconds tops. His tablet was gone, swept away by the storm. *I don't need it anymore anyway.* Nolan moved to the edge and hung down, swinging his feet until he found the ramp.

Dropping back into the ship, he took a moment to let his heart slow down as he gasped through the anxiety of what he'd just done. *I survived. That's good enough for me.* Nolan returned to the cockpit and restored power to the instrument panel. The flickering stopped but it was clear some of them were slow in gathering data.

That would be worse if I was trying to land down here. Nolan powered up the engines and closed the ramp. Strapping in, he sent a message to Cassie about the Tol'An vessels he saw. They might've already known but if not, the heads-up would definitely help. The second set of ships, he hadn't seen so it could be worse than he knew.

Either way, there was nothing Nolan could do on the ground. He lifted off and jammed the throttle forward, hurling himself back toward orbit. *Good luck, guys. I don't envy you down here.*

***

Anna sent the call to Raptor for help and they committed to getting to her as fast as they could. She would be with her own squadron shortly but the enemies chasing her were gaining. Even at full speed with afterburners, she still could only barely keep out in front of them.

"We're on our way to you," Preston said. "My computer suggests we'll meet up a good fifteen seconds before they can start shooting."

"I love it when we cut things close."

Preston chuckled. "This isn't really that close. I mean, we could slow down and get there with five seconds to spare if you'd rather."

"Knock it off." Anna checked her scanner and noted that Raptor would be there in one minute. They would be evenly matched after having to send one of theirs back for repairs. Unfortunately, the enemy weapons proved to be particularly nasty and her compute had yet to come up with a solution to charge the shields.

She had hoped Jonny would contact them back by then with some information. When she could let up on the throttle and breathe in anything other than short gasps, she'd reach out to the Gnosis for an update. Until then, all she could do was concentrate on forward motion, on keeping away from her attackers.

The scanner made them seem terribly close. She was reminded of something she saw in her childhood, a mirror in her grandfather's old car. It had a sticker that said *objects in mirror are closer than they appear*. They had always looked crazy close to her.

Her computer played the role this time. The enemy would be firing if they were as close as she felt in her gut. Even with the blips appearing on her screen, she had to ignore them and trust that Preston's estimate was right. They'd arrive in a moment, throwing themselves into another dogfight.

Ahead of her, she saw light from the thrusters of her unit. When they came into visual range, her confidence increased. The closest enemy ship to her seemed to be in the middle of their formation. It might've even been their squadron leader. Anna decided that was her target, the one she'd focus on when she spun around.

"Looks like we're about twelve seconds apart," Anna said. "I'm going to flip around and engage."

"Is that a good idea?" Preston asked. "Ten seconds can be an eternity in combat."

"Yeah, I think it'll be fine." Anna killed the afterburners and jammed the flight stick to the left. Maneuvering thrusters compelled her around, even as she continued in the direction of her unit. As she came around, she opened up, firing her weapons blindly at the enemy. They didn't flinch as she had hoped, and maintained their formation.

Okay, if that didn't move you ... Anna engaged her rear thrusters and charged toward them. *I* will *get your attention*. She let her computer attempt to grab a lock on her target but started firing before it could get a tone. The enemy fighters finally broke their formation, all but the one in the front who seemed intent on playing chicken.

This happens far more often than I'd like. Anna fired again but decided against testing the resolve of her opponent. Knowing her luck, the bastard wanted to ram her. Veering hard to the left, she engaged her top thrusters, allowing her to maneuver and take a shot at her target's flank while flying by him.

The pressure from the maneuver was only partially absorbed by her inertial dampeners. Anna's head ached as the weapons engaged, slapping the shields of her targets and splashing against them. He spun around, entering the dogfight with her in a graceful turn.

Anna righted herself, and moved in a straight path, parallel to his. Neither of them had a firing solution but as they started turning and spinning, it became apparent they were in for some work. All around them, weapons blasted through the darkness of space. Radio chatter indicated the constant rush of combat.

Anna focused on her task, letting herself fall into a zone of pure instinct. It might take some luck to survive the encounter, but she decided to rely on skill and training first. At least for so long as it took Raptor to join the party. *Hurry up, guys. We need to wrap this up.*

Chapter 8

Heat received an upload from Cassie of a basic floor plan for the facility. The kiosk they found contained a map used by the different vendors to get around to the places they were authorized for. While the off-limits areas were not called out by name, they were dark sections on the overall layout.

He examined it on his HUD, puzzling out that to get to the control room, they would need to go up. There was an elevator as well as a flight of stairs they could take. He led them to the stairway and frowned at the narrow corridor leading up. They could fit single file in the power armor but even that would be tight.

"I'll lead the way," Heat said. "Gillet, take up the rear with Agent Alexander directly in front of you. Come on." He proceeded inside, moving upward. He reached the landing and turned the corner. They needed to go up four floors to reach their destination. He doubted they would encounter opposition until they were closer.

"Guys," Cassie spoke over the com, trying to keep her voice down. "I just got a message from Nolan. We've got Tol'An incoming."

Heat was about to reply when Fielding came on the line. "I've got some bad news. Tol'An forces are on route to your position. Looks like they know about the prize and want to be involved. However, the good news is the Pahxin are sending some aid. But ..."

"Yeah," Heat muttered. "I knew that was coming."

"Well ... It's just the Tol'An will be there first. Still, it'll take them some time to establish a perimeter and get into the facility so you should be fine. What's your current status?"

"Heading up the stairs to get to the control room," Heat said. "We'll be there soon and will probably have another engagement. I'm guessing they've locked down the sensitive parts of the facility. I'd like to know how the Tol'An got here. Did we have another traitor tip them off? If so, I think it's time to do a loyalty test."

"The signal!" Cassie shouted. She winced when Heat glared over the rail at her. "Sorry, I didn't mean to ... Anyway, when we first arrived, there was a weird signal that Salina and I found. We couldn't isolate it before it turned off, but it definitely came from the facility. Maybe the traitor isn't ours. Maybe someone from Kalrawv is working for the Tol'An."

"That would make me feel better," Fielding said, "in a way."

"Sir?" Gillet chimed in. "Gunny? Maybe we can worry about all that when we're done taking the facility?"

"Quite right," Fielding replied. "I'll mark this down for command to look into. You guys stay safe and finish the mission. Keep me informed of your progress."

Heat achieved the final landing and the door immediately opened, sliding aside from proximity. If someone had been waiting on the other side, they would've been able to shoot him. There was no taking cover, no avoiding contact but fortunately, the Kalrawv security picked a different spot for their defense.

He took a quick scan of the hallway, noting it took a ninety-degree turn not twenty feet left and right. He stepped out and moved to the left first, pressing against the wall. "Stack on the other side," Heat muttered on the com. "Break up into two groups and we'll cover both directions. It seems to link up to the main hallway on the opposite side of the stairs."

There was no being sneaky. Every step in the power armor echoed from contact with the metal floor. For this reason, it didn't matter that they hurried. When they arrived at the next hallway, Heat and Gillet faced one another with the gap only a foot away between them. The telltale wheezing of the sonic blasters filled the air.

Yellow beams struck the wall, suppressive fire to keep them from advancing. "Grenades," Heat said, popping his. Gillet followed suit and they chucked them down the way, compelling the explosives with the assistance of the hydraulics.

Heat counted down in his head before the explosives went off, two quick flashes before going dark. The shooting didn't slow. *We must not have gotten them far enough.* He crouched and risked a quick glance, noting his targets were held up on the opposite side of a door at the end of the hallway.

"We're going to have to go bigger," Heat said. "Cassie, get back to the stairs. This … has the potential to go wrong." There wasn't enough room for more than two of them to initiate his plan.

"What're we going to do?" Gillet asked.

"Rockets."

"That'll make an impression."

"A big one hopefully." Heat drew a deep breath. "You ready?"

"As I'll ever be."

"We have to lean just enough so they don't hit the wall." Heat prepared himself and inched around the corner, launching his rocket. The thrust carried it swiftly down the hall, followed closely by Gillet's.

Two yellow blasts came close enough to Heat's shoulder that he swore he felt the heat from them. It was an illogical thought, an impossible notion but it made him dart back into his cover, heart racing. He knew what those weapons could do to a man, even in power armor. He didn't want to experience it firsthand.

The resulting explosion of the rockets made the floor shake. Kalrawv security forces began screaming, some shouting incoherently. Heat psyched himself to risk another glance. A massive section of the wall beside the door had been broken open, revealing circuitry beneath. The other attack hit the ceiling, leaving wires hanging down.

At least one man died in the attack. Bits of his body were scattered across the floor. Others seemed to be withdrawing, shouting for their fellows to fallback. They still held the tactical advantage, but the resulting explosions must've been enough to break their morale. Perhaps they didn't know how many times the marines could do it.

And technically, they could shell them for a while but if they were hiding out in the control room, then there was a risk of destroying their equipment. That would make hunting for the Orb all the more difficult.

"I'm moving up," Heat announced. "Get ready to follow. The room ahead looks large enough for us to spread out."

"I should go." Gillet didn't speak up fast enough. Heat was already in the hallway with his rifle aimed in the event someone poked their head around the corner. He hustled, his heavy footsteps echoing around him. As he reached the door, he noted that the security forces had abandoned the room.

A woman cowered in a corner nearby and he aimed at her. She lifted her hands, eyes closed as tears soaked her cheeks. "Please!" She shouted. "I'm ... I'm unarmed!"

"Get down here," Heat said. "Room's secure. There's an unarmed civilian scared out of her mind. She might be able to help."

The other marines came spilling into the room, securing the area. There were two other doors and they stacked up, acting as guards. Cassie entered next, assessing the situation from the entrance before cautiously moving in. "Oh God ..." She stepped over something, sneering. Heat had stepped on some body part when he entered.

He understood her reaction.

"I'll get on the terminal," Cassie said. "This place is a mess."

The woman spoke, "The other ... the man ... that ... that ... thug."

"What're you talking about?" Cassie asked. "What other man?"

"He came in here ... killed Dak ... I thought he was going to kill me too but he ... he didn't. He knocked me out. Security forces ... found me." She choked on her sobs. Cassie approached her, crouching. "He used the terminal, they said."

"Crap," Heat grumbled. "Tol'An, right? That sounds like one of their operatives causing trouble, don't you think?"

Cassie nodded. "Very likely." She touched the woman on the shoulder, making her jump. "I'm not going to hurt you. What was Kalrawv doing on this planet?"

"Resource ... acquisition."

Cassie tilted her head. "I don't think that's the whole truth, is it? Look at the attention this place suddenly grabbed. How long have you all been here?"

"I don't know ... I mean, I've been here for a while and I think they surveyed the planet half a year ago. Something happened recently. They doubled the mining crews and really started to strip this place. It's like ... there was a crazy deadline or something." She shrugged. "I genuinely don't know why."

"Sounds like they knew about it," Heat said. "We don't have time to mess with her. Get on the terminal, Cassie. Get this show moving."

Cassie stood and nodded. She hesitated for a long moment, examining the woman before turning to the console. "Maybe I can find out what he searched for." She tapped the console and cursed. "He seems to have wiped his activities. Damn it!"

"I can help." The woman stood up, drawing a couple of aimed rifles in her direction. She winced and held up her hands. "No really! I'm happy to assist. I saw what he did to Dak ... It was terrible. I swore I was next. I'll help you figure ... whatever you want out. Please, just ... let me try?"

Heat turned to Cassie who shrugged. "I can do it without her, but her help would make it quicker."

"My name's Jayla ... and I know these systems better than anyone. He might've wiped the front end of his search but there's a backup. I can bring it up and save you a lot of time."

Heat grumbled, "Don't even think about revealing our location to your buddies, lady. I don't have any patience for foolishness."

"Believe me," Jayla said. "I have no desire to push anyone today. I just want to make it out of here alive."

Cassie stepped aside, watching as Jayla brought up a menu on the console. The woman frowned, drilling down until she found what she was looking for. "This is weird." She gestured. "He was looking for an energy reading that ... well ... I mean, I'm not exactly a scientist, but I've seen scans before."

"What's wrong with it?" Cassie looked. "Oh."

"What?" Heat prompted.

"It's the Orb's energy reading. He was scanning the planet for it and found it deep in one of the mine shafts. That's where you need to go to find it." Cassie tapped at the screen for a moment. "I've uploaded the location to your computers. All of you have the map now."

"You coming?" Heat asked.

"I think I should stay here and help from the control room."

Heat sighed. "You won't be safe ... Damn it. I'll leave someone behind. Vine. You're back up for Agent Alexander."

"Suits me," Vine replied.

"I'll lock the doors," Cassie said. "The ones you didn't destroy at least."

"Good enough." Heat gestured for the other marines to follow him. "We're moving out. Seems like we're about to be in a race."

Jayla lifted a hand, "I think I can help find that man who infiltrated the facility. That might help."

"There you go," Cassie said. "Jayla and I have some things to do as well. Be careful, Heat. There's probably a lot more enemies between you and that Orb."

"Nah, I'm sure it'll be a piece of cake." Heat shook his head. "See you soon."

***

Gizan arrived at the mine shaft in question, pausing when he noticed Kalrawv guards up ahead. He looked down on himself, noting the blood covering his clothes, hands and face. They hadn't noticed him yet so he called out for them not to shoot. Rushing forward, he put his hands over his head, throwing furtive glances behind him.

"Hold there!" One of the guards shouted. "What's going on?"

"I just barely survived!" Gizan cried. "I was in the control room when the invaders attacked. They slaughtered the others! It was an absolute massacre!"

"Is that what's going on up there?" The second guard spoke up. "We haven't heard anything over the com."

These fools don't even communicate! Gizan found it ridiculous. They must've been in total chaos. *This might work to my advantage.*

"They're coming down this way," Gizan replied, creeping ever closer to them. He only needed another couple feet to be in melee range. "They want something hidden in the shaft … some secret we didn't know about! I've come down here to check it out … to see if we have something to negotiate with."

"How so?" The guard on the left tilted his head. "Who are you anyway? What're you even doing down here?"

"I'm Oswald," Gizan said. He spoke the name as if he should've been well known. The guards turned to each other. That's when he struck, slamming his fist into the left man's throat and grabbing the other. They struggled for a moment before Gizan brought his target to the ground and snapped his neck.

The other gasped and sputtered, unable to speak. He stumbled back into the wall, trying to lift his weapon. Gizan aimed his own pistol and fired into the man's stomach. Internal organs burst and the man spit blood before dropping to the ground with a gory splatter.

Gizan hurried past them deeper into the mine shaft. His personal com began to chime and he checked. It was a scrambled channel from his Tol'An allies. He established a connection. "Speak."

"This is Commander Dalant. We have established ourselves on the planet but are currently engaged with Kalrawv forces. They seem to be using sonic weaponry. What is your status?"

"I am near the Trindisha," Gizan replied. "Use your ships to bombard the base where your opponents are and get down here as quickly as you can. I'm sending you a beacon now. We must make haste if we want to escape with this prize. The humans and the Pahxin military are here and will send reinforcements."

"Yes, some of our ships are engaged with Kalrawv and the Pahxin now," Dalant said. "They will hold them back while we accomplish our goal. I need to cut this contact while we attack the base. We will rendezvous as quickly as possible. Good luck, sir."

Gizan wondered how many ships they brought. They had a large threat out there to contend with, potent military forces that were well trained and dangerous. Ezria understood the value of the mission, the criticality of success. *Hopefully, he committed an appropriately sized force to make this happen.*

The entrance to the mine shaft was set with a metal floor but natural walls and ceiling. Beyond where the guards were stationed, the floor went away and he walked on uneven stone ground. Darkness closed in on him, but lights pounded into the walls provided illumination every twenty to thirty feet.

Gizan followed the tunnel as it descended. A small army could've easily traversed the area. The Kalwrav Group must've brought heavy equipment through, taking drills and the like into the deepest sections of the planet. Silence surrounded him, sucking up all the sound from his footsteps.

Where are all the miners? Gizan wondered if maybe he was wrong. Kalrawv might've simply been strip mining the world and getting out. But that didn't entirely make sense. There were plenty of places they could've exploited legally. Why bother out here? Was saving money that important?

Probably. Gizan rounded a corner and paused as the tunnel opened into a vast chamber. Digging machines were scattered about, treaded for travel over the difficult terrain. A prefabricated unit sat off to the left, probably for employee downtime. Lights lined the ceiling, wires laced between them while hanging down a good five feet.

Several Kalrawv agents occupied the opposite side of the room. They stood beside a wall, gesturing to it over and over again. Gizan checked his tablet, confirming that they were standing near the Trindisha. *They do know. And now, they're just trying to work out exactly what to do.*

They had options. If Kalrawv surrendered to the Pahxin, they could give up the rights to the Trindisha and probably walk away with little more than a slap to the wrist. However, they would also lose out on all that power. Surely, their higher ups sent them there for it. Failure for those corporate mercenaries was quite simply not allowed.

Much like Ezria, people tended to be executed for less.

They could always surrender to me, Gizan mused. The Tol'An didn't hide their presence. Kalrawv knew they had come and so they had to scramble if they wanted to walk away with anything at all. *I'm afraid I have nothing to offer them but a swift death. I doubt they're interested in accepting it.*

The guards spread out and rushed toward the edges of the room. They shouted to one another that each tunnel they passed was clear while tossing down something, likely a sensor probe to keep an eye on it. They'd be upon him shortly and he knew he needed to play up his role quickly or he'd have to kill even more men.

"What're you doing here?" One of the soldiers approached. "This is a restricted area!"

"Of course it is, you idiot," Gizan replied, pacing toward him. "I've come down here to ensure it stays that way. Do you have any idea what's going on up there? I'm assuming from the way you're moving so slowly, you don't. There are invaders in this facility and they're killing everyone! Civilians, security forces … It's bad."

"I don't recognize you." The soldier spoke tentatively, clearly unsure if he should be questioning the newcomer.

"Typical." Gizan shook his head. "I know why we're down here. If you don't let me pass, I won't be able to secure that prize for our higher ups. Do you want to fail? Be my guest, I'll be happy to throw your name out there when I'm asked who stopped me." He glared at him. "Who's in charge here anyway?"

"Narius." The soldier pointed back toward the man standing alone near the wall. "He's in command right now."

"I'll just go speak to him then." Gizan moved past the two soldiers, not bothering to look at them as he walked. Neither of them stopped him and instead locked down the passage he'd just come through. It made him smirk. *That worked out better than I could've hoped. If I play this right, these fools will keep this safe until my people arrive.* "Narius!"

The man looked up with a confused expression on his face. "Um ... who are you?"

"I'm in charge," Gizan said. "I know what's behind this wall and we're going to need to secure it. I've got the guards locking down the area up there so we should make haste. What's your plan to open this up?"

"Um ..." Narius looked around, pursing his lips. "To be honest, I was about to contact the Pahxin ship and ask them to stand down in exchange for whatever's in here. Our forces are being devastated. We cannot stand against that battleship. They've already taken out three of our destroyers and now, I've heard the Tol'An have arrived as well!"

"I'm not going to give up that easily," Gizan said. "I refuse to let you do so either. I will contact the Pahxin for us and delay them while we get this thing out. Perhaps we can smuggle it away while we negotiate." He shook his head. "You must be clever to get ahead in this organization, Narius. I'm disappointed in your lack of forethought."

"People are dying, sir," Narius replied. "How many lives is this thing worth? How many resources is the company willing to lose?"

"All of them," Gizan said. "Do you not realize this is a Trindisha? The government greedily held on to theirs until it was stolen. And they never even admitted there was a possibility of more. Now, we know there are and I'm planning on taking a promotion for turning this over to my superiors. You must make a choice."

"And what's that?" Narius asked.

"Whether you wish to rise with me," Gizan stepped closer, "or be held accountable for our failure."

Narius didn't have to consider the statement for long before he nodded emphatically. "Alright, I'm with you. What do we have to do?"

Gizan scanned the wall with his tablet and smirked. "Secure the device with some explosives. You gather them. Don't use the drills … you might damage it. I'll start delaying our adversaries now. Hurry. We may not have much time before their forces storm these mines and root us out but before then, I fully intend to have this on a ship leaving the system."

"I'm on it!" Narius rushed off and Gizan smiled, turning away. He engaged his communicator, reaching out to the Pahxin.

"Military vessel," he began, "this is the Kalrawv Group requesting parlay. Please respond."

***

Ulian gripped his seat as Erda took them through another round of evasive maneuvers. It didn't save them from all the shots this time, but with only four destroyers left, the damage done was minimal. The battleship remained the biggest threat but the Tol'An kept them busy on the opposite side of the battlefield.

Fighter wings reported some losses though not as heavy as initially expected. The biggest threat on the field likely came from the Kalrawv bombers, but they had now been taken out. The destroyers managed to cause structural damage on multiple sides of the Stalwart but nothing too traumatic.

It seemed likely they would call the engagement a victory soon enough.

Providing the ground action goes according to plan ... and the Tol'An don't pull anything unexpected.

"Erda," Morala said, "close on our targets. Initiate full thrust and fire as we go."

Ulian's eyes widened and he turned to her. "What's the tactic here?"

"I intend to finish off the destroyers and be in position to finish off the battleship," Morala replied. "While they're distracted with the Tol'An, I intend to wrap this entire engagement up so we can focus our attention on the new threat."

Ulian considered how to respond, wondering if he even needed to. It wasn't a tactic he would've chosen, but he saw the merit. And he did give her operational command for a reason. After a moment of reconciling his thoughts to the choice, he merely nodded and leaned back in his seat, prepared to see the results.

Erda engaged the engines, pushing them toward their objective at a rapid pace. Morala warned the fighters to move before they arrived, letting them know the Stalwart would be plowing right through their position. The Kalrawv vessels turned tail and tried to pull away, moving toward the Tol'An.

I suppose they've decided they don't have the firepower, Ulian thought. *Maybe this was the right call after all.*

Viran cleared her throat, "I have a Kalrawv representative from the planet on the line. They'd like to discuss terms for the surrender of …" She paused. "A Trindisha."

Morala cursed. "Put them on speaker, please."

"I'll take this," Ulian replied. "This is Ulian Hataran of the Stalwart. State what you want."

"My name is Gizan and I am contacting you because I realize why you are here. This is an unlawful attain to claim something we did not even know was present. However, we would like to live so we are prepared to turn it over to you in return for leaving our remaining vessels alone."

"We can simply take it either way," Ulian said. "And I believe your battle commander suggested we were going to fight when we spoke before. They don't appear to be ready to stand down … but they might be on their way out. Besides, you have another problem besides us. Even if I accepted your deal, it would not be a simple trade of your lives for the device."

"Then perhaps you should do your duty as a government official," Gizan replied, "and protect us against those terrorists. I believe even now you have men on this world which are about to confront the Tol'An. Many of my people have been slain for no reason other than your greed to steal."

"You know the law." Ulian scowled as he spoke. "You did not acquire a license for this operation, you have several unregistered silhouettes, illegal weapons ... and on top of it all, you expect me to believe you had no knowledge of the Trindisha. We may be many things in the military but stupid is not one of them. Tell me the truth."

"All I know is that you have the blood of innocent people on your hands!" Gizan shouted. "You have threatened and bullied us, and we are now making an honest offer but you're throwing ... legalities and other nonsense in our faces! Well, that is *not* going to fly in a court of law, sir!"

"I feel you're stalling us," Ulian said. "But really, you shouldn't be. Right now, we are charging your final ships with the intention of finishing this battle once and for all. If you have a real offer, then make it. Otherwise, I'm going to close this line down and you can surrender to the ground forces when they converge on your position."

"You cannot do this!" Gizan cried. "For the sake of *honor,* you should stay your hand!"

"I believe you have a short period of time before our people arrive," Ulian answered. "I suggest you find a way to show them you surrender so they do not fire. The choice is yours. We will speak again when you are safely within a cell on your way back to the home world for a trial of your own. Hataran out."

Ulian cut the connection and turned to Morala. "Sorry about that. Please, continue the operation."

"With pleasure, sir." Morala turned to Erda. "Open fire."

Chapter 9

The lights flashed on the Gnosis bridge as the strange beam struck them again. Zach got them moving swiftly, the ship lurching backward away from the assault. They pulled away and the beam disappeared. Desmond guessed they saved themselves several seconds of continuous damage by moving.

"I was right," Salina announced. "They have to calculate the range and there's not a lot of margin for error there."

"Excellent," Desmond replied. "Damage report?"

"Minor hull scorching," Salina said. "Casualty report is coming in. Those who were closest to that section are reporting radiation burns. Shields are down to thirty percent on the bow. I'm diverting power to charge them, but the emitters are having trouble. Webber's sending a team now."

Desmond peered at the screen, staring intently at their opponent. They'd blasted them several times, giving as good as they were getting. "Vincent, do you think we're ready to send the bombers in?"

Vincent stared at his terminal's screen for a long moment before letting out a sigh. "Probably. Even if their shields are over thirty percent, the concussion damage alone should be enough to finish them off. And if we have them launch everything?" He shrugged. "That would level an unshielded space station. It'll at least give them something to think about."

"Order them in." Desmond pointed at Zach. "Keep hitting that ship. Salina, I want a report on how our fighters are doing, both right here and with the Stalwart. Get me some data, folks. Those people on the surface are going to want some support soon and if we're not in a position to give it to them, we'll be risking the mission."

***

Flight Lieutenant Micah Zane didn't mind having to lead the bomber squadron, but he had hoped Nolan would have joined them already. They waited on the edge of the battle, essentially watching as the destroyer and the Gnosis went toe to toe. The chaos of fighter combat exploded before them and they simply had to hold back.

Glory to the fighter jockeys. Micah couldn't put much conviction behind the snark. He didn't really want to be out there dogfighting with the enemy, especially when he heard the radio chatter. Listening to them talk about flashing blasts that knocked out shields did not sound like his idea of a good time.

Nor would it be particularly glorious to be blown away by one of those crazy bastards, even if that was a possibility when they were finally scrambled into action to do their part.

"Lieutenant Zane," Vincent Bowman's voice filled his cockpit. "I am authorizing you to attack. Attack the enemy vessel with everything you've got. Hit it with all ordnance. Copy?"

"Copy, Commander." Micah bit his lip. "That's an awful lot of firepower ... We need to ensure everyone's well away from that blast. The shockwave alone could be devastating."

"Understood," Vincent replied. "I'm giving orders to the pilots now. You'll have some escorts, but they won't be able to meet you until you're half way there. Godspeed, Lieutenant. Bowman out."

Micah leaned back in his seat, sweat coating his back. He half expected they wouldn't be called into action, that the conflict would be over without their intervention. The thought of hitting the destroyer with everything made him anxious. It meant the Gnosis bridge crew may not be confident they could do enough damage on their own to take it out.

The concussion alone would be enough to put a hurt on the thing. If the planet wasn't already in a terrible way, the bombs might've pushed the atmospheric interference to a new level of dangerous. None of that mattered just then. The order came. He and his people had a job to do.

"Rhino," Micah cleared his throat when the word didn't come out with the force he intended. "Rhino Squadron, we have been ordered to hit the enemy vessel with everything we've got. Each of us will fire our entire payload at the vessel and withdraw to safety. I'll take the lead, form up on me."

"Sir," Lieutenant Mariah Pine spoke, "is that going to be safe? How are we going to get out of there ahead of the shockwave with so many bombs going off at once?"

"Won't be a problem," Officer Deanne Stewart answered. "Once we deploy, we spin around and hit the afterburners. We'll have a good ten seconds before the bombs go off and another thirty before they could possibly catch up. That's plenty of time to reach a minimal safe distance. I'd be more worried about the planet … and the fighters."

"Planet's already hosed," Micah said. He engaged his engines, flying directly for their target. "And the fighters will move. Besides, they're more nimble than we are. We've got this. Get your turrets on and your shields on full. This is going to be one hell of a trip and depending on how it goes, the return won't be much fun either."

"What about Nolan?" Mariah asked. "Can we expect him to join the party?"

"I haven't been able to reach him on the com," Micah replied. "And God knows that interference is messing with it." *I hope he made it okay. That weather would've been enough to put anyone down hard.* "Regardless, we'll keep an eye out and let him in on the action. I don't think he'd want to miss this."

Yeah ... fat chance.

***

Nolan raced toward orbit, just clearing the cloud coverage when his communicator started working. The chatter involved the nearby fighters and the bombers moving into position to deploy against the destroyer. *Well, at least they got to do something, I suppose.* He checked his gauges and everything seemed to be functioning still.

Small favors.

"Nolan?" Vincent's voice crackled in his ears. "Can you hear me? Are you there?"

"Commander," Nolan replied. "I had some challenges on the surface and I'll need to make a landing. Lightning took out a relay."

"Are you combat effective?"

Nolan hesitated to answer. His shields were functional. He kept them on to hold the panel in place. Weapons were also online. "I would cautiously say *yes* but I was literally coming in for repairs."

"I'm afraid I need you to redirect toward the surface," Vincent said. "I need you to help with escort duty. There are some Pahxin fighters but they're calling for backup … You're the closest ship to them."

"Escort." Nolan's brows lifted. "You have to be kidding, sir. Maneuverability down there is terrible for the best of ships and I'm flying a big ass boat. What happened to Raptor?"

"They're backing up Charger right now."

"God damn it." Nolan sighed. "Yes, sir. I'll head back there now."

"Get down there, ensure the transports land and come home. Thank you."

"Yeah, I get it." Nolan flipped around and flew toward the planet, shaking his head. *This is an absolutely terrible idea.* He prepared himself for the winds again, hoping he would have a better time of it on his descent. As the ship started shaking and he had to fight the controls, he cursed under his breath. *Yep, still a really bad idea!*

Shields held through the worst of the turbulence but far more important was that the panel remained in place. He wondered if it might be able to come loose despite the shields but even if it did, his bypass remained functional. Breaking through the clouds, the surface burst into view some distance below him, a sight he never wanted to see again.

"Okay …" Nolan clicked on the open com channel. "Pahxin fighter escort, this is Rhino One requesting a position. I've been ordered to provide an escort. Please respond."

It took him three tries before someone finally responded.

"Human ship," a woman's stiff voice returned, "I am sending you a ping. We are under heavy attack by Kalrawv mercenaries. Any assistance would be much appreciated. We have two full loads of soldiers who need to get onto that facility."

"Understood." Nolan checked his scanner and noted he could be there in less than thirty seconds, weather permitting. "I'm fairly close. See you in a moment. Please don't shoot at the lumbering bomber heading in your direction, okay?"

"You are on our friend or foe list already. Good luck."

Hope I don't need it. Nolan winced as another gust of wind nearly tossed him thirty feet off course. He corrected, working the throttle of his thrusters to fight the gale. Drawing the stick back, he climbed to buy himself some altitude, but the air wasn't any better up there.

Weapon fire lit up the horizon and he saw the fight he was about to get into. The shuttles barreled down on the facility with all the tenacity and stubbornness of bulls. Nolan counted five in all and they were being harassed by nearly eight fighters. The four escorts struggled against the weather and their attackers, flying erratically in the conditions.

How much good am I going to do? Nolan thought. The Pahxin had to have sent more than four ships to protect their soldiers. *How many did they lose before I was asked to help?* Asking the question would've been in bad taste. He needed to ensure those soldiers made it to their destination, regardless of circumstance.

The blasts from the enemy ships came in quick flashes. They didn't fire without a decent solution. Evaluating it didn't help much but it passed the few seconds it would take for him to get there. He elected to go in below them, jamming the after burners to plow through the difficult air pockets and give him the best chance to cause some damage.

Nolan cranked on the automated attack program, feeding it the enemy pilots as targets. When he drew close enough, the guns kicked on, blasting away as he lumbered beneath them. Pahxin pilots darted all around him, little more than blurs from their speed. The enemy scattered, and the shuttles kept going.

"How much time do we have to buy?" Nolan asked, climbing as he finished his attack run. One of the enemy ships decided to follow him. His turret rewarded them with a constant stream of fire, forcing them into evasive maneuvers that drove them off after only a few moments.

"One minute to landing," a Pahxin voice came back. "We're almost there."

Christ, that's forever. Nolan banked and came around, speeding back toward the others. The wind caught one of his allies, tossing it into the facility. The ship exploded in an instant, leaving a giant hole in the ceiling of that particular wing. *Holy shit! That guy didn't even have a chance to eject!*

Nolan worried about crashing down there before there was gunfire. Something struck the back of his ship as the turret engaged once again. Minor shield damage didn't slow him down but the enemy kept at it, clipping away at his defenses. This opponent remained dedicated to takin him down, even to the point that they risked the blasts from his guns.

Six shots from the turret ripped through the enemy, cutting into the nose and cockpit. A massive fire exploded from the seams as the fighter went down, smacking the ground hard enough to send a plume of dust and smoke high into the air. *Seven left ... three escorts, me and a bunch of shuttles with crappy weapons. Lovely.*

"One down." Nolan saw another flash nearby as one of the Kalrawv vessels exploded in a spectacular show of purple and green.

A wall of gray clouds roiled in the east, turning into a swirling vortex of a massive storm. Nolan estimated it to be no more than a hundred miles away and it moved swiftly. The wind and rain combined into a funnel, a tornado tearing up the soil and dancing in their direction. *What would that do to the facility?*

An alarm went off, pulling his attention to his right. He banked hard to avoid a collision with one of the enemies, and his turret blasted away as the ship flew past. Leveling out, he flew over the shuttles, fending off the attacking ships that darted all around them.

He noted another Pahxin loss, cutting the escorts down to two other flyers and his bomber. Kalrawv still had five flyers up there, plenty to destroy those shuttles and finish off the escorts. Nolan's turrets drove them off temporarily and when they returned, they seemed focused on him. It made sense. He represented the biggest threat.

His armor and shields were tough, and his weapons could get them from any angle. It made up for his relatively poor maneuverability. As one of his blasts clipped one of the enemies in the rear, cutting right through their shields and causing massive damage, he knew they'd be directing all their efforts on him momentarily.

"I recommend you guys land ASAP and breach a wall," Nolan said. "When they finally dedicate everything to me, I won't last long. In fact … I'm going to lead them off to buy you a little breathing room. Escorts, remain with the shuttles and wish me luck."

He yanked the stick back and jammed the throttle forward, hurling himself upward. The Tornado to the east continued to meander in their direction. It was an opportunity. The funnel itself would be far too dangerous to fly into but his ship was big enough to survive the turbulence *around* it.

Banking to the east, he flew off toward the storm, aiming directly for it. It would take less than a minute to get there but he banked gradually to ensure he'd give it a wide berth. The Kalrawv pilots continued to chase him, knowing full well that if they returned to their original quarry, Nolan would come right back.

Perhaps they knew they failed to keep the Pahxin soldiers away from their base and merely wanted some revenge. The shuttle escorts didn't pursue them, but remained close to their charges, letting Nolan lead them off. Oddly enough, they weren't taking shots at him as they followed.

Is that a limitation of their flashy weapons? Nolan didn't have time to appreciate it before one of them caught him in the aft, cutting his shields down to thirty percent.

Scans offered some level of predictive analysis concerning how the storm would move but Nolan knew he couldn't rely on it. The funnel would go in whatever direction it felt like, indulging total chaos. Keeping the dark mass in his peripheral vision, Nolan banked gently away, kicking on the bottom thrusters to give him some additional distance.

One of the fighters tried to take advantage of his motion, swooping in to take a shot at his underside. The turbulence from the funnel proved too much for the smaller craft, grabbing it and spinning it directly into the funnel. It spun around, torn at unimaginable speeds, surely enough to kill the pilot.

The ejection pod burst free and the ship was crushed a moment later.

Nolan pulled up, hitting the afterburners. The storm raged behind him now, but the winds made his ascent a shaky nightmare. More shots connected with his rear, cutting through his shields. Instruments went haywire as the panel he'd repaired earlier came free. The bypass dropped.

Good thing I'm going up, I guess. Nolan spun in place, hoping his turret would be enough to drive them off. They continued following him, dodging his attacks while chipping away at his defenses.

"Anyone out there," Nolan spoke over the com. "I could *really* use some help right about now. I'm just about to break atmosphere and I've got some seriously persistent pricks all over my ass. Please respond."

Interference filled the speakers with static. He'd received a message from the Gnosis when he reached that altitude. *Come on, folks.* Turbulence settled down, but another shot from his pursuers made the ship shake violently. "Guys, seriously, I need a hand. Any fighter out here, respond!"

Despair grabbed Nolan as more alarms went off. He couldn't even check the damage due to his scanner being down. The turret fell silent, no longer blasting away at the targets behind him. They had no hindrance to end him now, nothing preventing them from continuing to hound him straight through to their final shot.

He eyeballed the ejection handle, but he wasn't high enough to avoid going right back down to the planet. Another few moments would make all the difference. It would mean he would at least be found by search and rescue rather than be killed by some rampaging storm on one of the God forsaken continents below him.

Weapons exploded in front of him as two fighters sped so fast it made his head spin.

"Relax," Lieutenant Dylan Ball replied to him. He was Raptor Two and had been assigned for air support on the planetary operation. "We've got your back, buddy. Just keep on with your current course and we'll take care of your pals. They're already breaking away. I guess they don't want to play with even odds."

"No, it didn't seem like it," Nolan muttered. "Thank you, guys. You have no idea how good it is to see you."

"Sorry it took so long to get here. Your com must be messed up. We heard you, but you must not have heard us. We asked you to bank left."

"Yeah, believe me, I've got a lot of problems on my end right now." Nolan redirected toward the Gnosis, ready to dock. "See you guys back at the ship. Thanks again!" Violence broke behind him and he had no doubt he owed both pilots his life. As he broke atmosphere, he redirected to the Gnosis. He'd make it up to them on the trip back.

That was a promise.

***

Micah winced as a blast struck his left side, causing his shields to flash so brightly it left tracers in his eyes. He blinked several times, trying to clear his vision but it only barely worked. They were close to their target but the Kalrawv pilots altered their course, laying into the bombers as soon as they were within range.

Even with Charger and Raptor swarming them, the enemy worked hard to keep the larger ships away. Turrets blared and pilots sacrificed their lives in an effort to hold the bombers off but they just couldn't do enough damage to break through their defenses. Deanne took the worst of it, but even at twenty-percent shields, they still had her armor to contend with.

The targeting computer provided a countdown before they needed to deploy their weapons. Micah swore it was moving in slow motion but as it dropped below two thousand kilometers, he felt a sudden sense of urgency. The enemy ships began to frenzy about them, like riled up bees.

"Watch out," Nolan said, "these maniacs might be crazy enough to ram someone. Be ready to maneuver. We're firing in …" He checked the scanner. "Less than twenty seconds. Be prepared."

One of the enemy ships nearly clipped his nose and he instinctually dove. The maneuver might've saved his life, he couldn't be sure but it also benefited the enemy, buying the destroyer another few moments. A little more effort on his opponent's part might've put him off for half a minute.

What good will that do for them? God only knows.

Did they have a plan? Something that would save them if they only had another minute? Micah doubted it and as he deployed his bombs, sending them hurtling through space toward their target, he figured they would never know what the enemy hoped to achieve with their last-ditch effort.

"Weapons clear!" Micah shouted, flipping around and hitting the afterburners. A new number appeared on his scanner, indicating how far he was away from the target. It was in the red, meaning he was too close. The goal was to get to green and they should've had plenty of time.

The others called out their deployments before racing to join him. The next two minutes would determine a great many things, not the least of which whether or not they blew the enemy destroyer ... and if they'd survive the attempt. Somewhere along the way, the enemy fighters disengaged or were destroyed by allied ships.

At least they weren't harassing the bombers anymore.

"Gnosis, this is Rhino Two. We have deployed bombs and are fleeing the area." Micah paused as two Raptor pilots dashed by them, screaming toward the planet surface. *Yeah, I wish we were that fast.* He checked his scanner and caught sight of Nolan's ship, Rhino One, just on the verge of breaking atmosphere.

Micah worked his communicator. *How did I not hear anything come through from him?* "I ... *really* ... some help ... now. Break atmosphere ... seriously ... pricks ... ass. Respond!"

"Hey!" Micah called but his computer let him know his message didn't go through. He didn't have the luxury of messing with it just at that moment. Instead, he focused his attention on getting away from the destruction. Clearly the two Raptor pilots were on route to help Nolan out.

We have to just focus on ourselves right now.

***

"Bombs are away," Vincent announced. "Impact in less than thirty seconds."

Desmond merely nodded, staring at the screen. The enemy destroyer kept trying to close the distance between them, but Zach did a great job of staying out of range, ensuring they couldn't hit them with their special weapon for long. On the flip side, the Gnosis pounded their ship with continuous barrages of firepower, but it wasn't enough to finish them off.

Hopefully all those bombs will at least give them a damn head ache.

He needed a better understanding of enemy defenses, or at least the engineers did. Their weapons required some tweaking to make these engagements even. Without tricks and maneuverability, the Gnosis would've been outmatched. If the bombers didn't pull off a victory for them, they'd end up needing the Stalwart to step in.

Our weapons hit pretty hard when we get through their damn shields, but those barriers are incredible. Desmond turned to Salina. "Do we have a report from our fighters? How did we do?"

"I'm still waiting to hear back from everyone," Salina said. "Mustang One was shot down ... His pod ejected but the interference is making it impossible for me to get through to him. I have his beacon for search and rescue. Raptor Four is also down. Those are the ones I know for sure. Rhino One is on route back to the ship for repairs."

"He's probably pretty grumpy," Vincent muttered. "I had to divert him to help support the Pahxin ground force arrival on the planet. They were having a rough time."

"Understood." Desmond tapped his com and brought up Fielding. "Report. How're things on the planet? Have you heard from Agent Alexander?"

"Sir, our people know where the Orb is located and are on their way to secure it. Agent Alexander is in the control room, providing backup support. We've had some casualties …" Fielding paused. "They have a nasty set of weapons down there that we're dealing with but otherwise, I don't foresee any additional complications at this time."

"Thank you." Desmond frowned. "Let me know if anything else comes up and especially once we have the Orb in our possession." He flipped off the com. "Anyone know how the Stalwart is doing? I'm shocked the Tol'An have left us alone and stayed on that side of the system."

Vincent explained, "The Kalrawv ships are pinned between the Stalwart and the Tol'An but they seem to be holding their own. At least … the battleship is. There's only one destroyer left. Allied pilots have devastated the enemy fighter squadrons but at a cost. Pahxin command is reporting at least a dozen casualties on their side."

Desmond was about to say something else when the screen caught his attention. Their opponent picked up speed, racing toward them. Bombs struck the side, plowing into the shields in a devastating display of bright lights and explosions. Even as the shields went down and the hull opened up, the vessel continued forward.

"Direct hits …" Vincent's voice trailed off. "Oh …"

"Zach," Desmond said, but the pilot waved his hand.

"I see what he's doing." Zach grunted. "This is going to be unpleasant." He tapped the console and spoke to the ship. "This is your pilot speaking. Please grab something and hold tight. This ride's about to get bumpy." He ran his fingers along his touch screen, grabbed the edge of the console and slapped something in the center.

The ship lurched, and Desmond flopped against Vincent from the sudden motion of it. Pressure held him in place for almost ten seconds before he was thrust backward, pinned into the cushion of his seat. "What the hell are you doing, Zach?"

"Getting us out of here," Zach replied. "If he means to ram us, he's going to have to find some speed out of that wreck. Otherwise, I'm not granting him a parting shot today."

The view screen switched to a rear camera, showing the destroyer barreling down on them. Fire billowed from its sides, great globes of orange and red, bursting from the seams as it lumbered closer. A thought crept into Desmond's mind of some fantastic beast, letting loose its fury through flames and rage.

"Their reactor is going critical," Salina said. "Not from the damage we did either. It looks like they've set it to go up like that."

"That's definitely a parting shot," Desmond replied. "What's minimum safe distance?"

"We'll get there," Zach called out. "Order the pilots to hall ass away though. The shockwave wouldn't make them feel particularly good about the situation."

Vincent got on the com and gave the order, straining against the continuous speed holding them firmly in their seats. The destroyer began to tumble, their engines failing. All at once, it went up, a massive explosion that blanked out the camera. Desmond held his breath ... The ship rattled wildly and he was nearly tossed from his seat.

"He's gone!" Zach shouted. "Damage to rear thrusters ... seems to be minimal. I've still got maneuvering."

"Salina, damage report!" Desmond shouted the words, gritting his teeth against the constant g force holding him in place.

"Minimal damage to housing," Salina announced. "Shields are completely down. Emitters are burned out. Relays throughout the ship have also sparked. We'll need some minor repairs before we can enter hyperspace. Engineering will gather an ETA when we've slowed down and they can get around their department again."

"I think we're good now, Zach," Desmond said. "Slow us down. Get the pilots on board ASAP and send a message to the Stalwart. We're down to ground ops at this point and if they need some help …" He considered their damage and what they'd been through. If they wanted to leave quickly, they couldn't get back in the mix. Not without tremendous risk.

"Sir?" Salina asked. "What do you want me to tell them?"

"They might be out of luck," Desmond replied. He didn't like it but he had to think of the rest of the mission. The most important part: getting the Orb back home. If they couldn't manage that, then everything else would've been for nothing. Attacking the Kalrawv, landing on the planet, engaging the Tol'An. "But if they need us … we'll do what we can."

Survival first, mission second. That's what set them apart from both the Kalrawv Group and the Tol'An.

Chapter 10

Cassie caught the conversation between Gizan and the Stalwart but a security block prevented her from intervening. She put a camera on the mining section where the Kalrawv forces were gathered and zeroed in on the speaker. Her eyes narrowed as she took him in and it dawned on her that she recognized him by description.

But Jayla interrupted. "That's him!" She shouted. "That's the man who killed Dak and nearly killed me! He must be the Tol'An infiltrator!"

The base alarm lit up, talking about intruders. *That seems a little late*, Cassie thought. "Shouldn't that have gone off when we got here?"

"I don't know why it's going off now." Jayla peered at another screen. "Oh … um … maybe it's those two groups."

Cassie looked and sighed. At least twenty Tol'An forces poured in at one point of the base and the Pahxin military, numbering around thirty, came from another. According to the schematics, they'd meet somewhere in the middle. When the marines arrived, most of the civilians were at work in different mine shafts around the facility.

Several of the miners left their post, moving directly into harm's way.

"Can we communicate with those people?" Cassie pointed. "Tell them they have to go back to their quarters or something?"

"I can try." Jayla started working the controls. "Something's jamming us … and they shouldn't be able to, considering how much control we have up here."

"Damn it!" Cassie turned to Vine. "I'm pretty sure the Tol'An we're talking about is the one who kidnapped Admiral Reach and the Pahxin ambassador. He's probably how the Tol'An got here but worse, he's pretending to be Kalrawv. He has *them* helping him! We have to warn Heat and the others."

"I will," Vine said, "but in all honesty, what's it matter? Whoever's down there is going to put up a fight."

"They're planting explosives," Jayla pointed out. "Look, they're putting charges on the wall."

"That's where … well … what we're looking for is behind that wall." Cassie checked the position of the marines. They were closing in but wouldn't be there for another several minutes. Reinforcements would be too busy to assist, and it was hard to get an accurate count of opposition in the mine. "Vine, can they handle whatever they find in there?"

"Those weapons are nasty," Vine replied. "Still … I think we'll be fine. We've got heavier gear than they do. And if they don't get that wall open, we'll definitely bust it down. One way or another."

"Wait, what??" Jayla cried. "Look! The Tol'An! They're … What are they doing?"

Cassie looked over her shoulder, noting that the Tol'An forces were darting into a maintenance tunnel. "Where's that go?"

"I honestly don't know," Jayla said. "I'm sure it goes to that mine though. Why else would they be heading down it? I suppose they could be planning to blow up the facility, I've heard they do that kind of thing … just straight murder innocent people? It happens all the time according to the vid feeds."

"No, I think they're here to back up this … Gizan guy." Cassie shook her head. "That's going to complicate the fight for our people." She turned to Vine. "None of them care about this area now. You should get down there and back them up. Or meet up with the Pahxin and give them a heads-up."

"I have orders to stay here," Vine said. "Work on the com and reach out to the Pahxin. I'll let Fielding and Heat know what we learned and see what they want me to do. Otherwise, I'm staying right here and protecting this room and you." He turned away to get on the com.

"Okay," Cassie muttered, "that's a soldier for you." She looked at Jayla. "We have access to the sensor relays, right? Can't we use those to counter all this … jamming?"

"Some of it is from your ship," Jayla replied. "That's going to be difficult to overcome. But internal jamming? From the Tol'An? Yes, I think I can." She hurried over to one of the consoles and popped it open. "I just need to bypass some of the security and safety measures ... That will give us access to what we need."

"Perfect!" Cassie tried to find the exact frequency the Tol'An was using to jam their signals. Once Jayla finished, they'd be able to cancel it out and hopefully have an easier time intercepting Kalrawv and Tol'An communications. Controlling the conversations would help settle the situation, even as the marines rushed into what would definitely be a final fight.

I hope Vine can get in contact with them, Cassie thought as she worked. *They're in for quite the surprise if they show up thinking they only have a few security personnel to deal with. At least the Tol'An weapons aren't as terrifying. That's a small consolation for the odds they'll be facing but reinforcements are on the way. Good luck, guys. We'll do what we can.*

***

Heat led the way for his team, hustling down a hallway that supposedly led to the mining tunnel in question. Sweat soaked his clothes to his body and his legs ached, despite the fact the armor provided so much assistance. They still had a fight on the way, a brawl he didn't anticipate would amount to much.

There couldn't be *that* many people waiting for them.

When Vine connected with him, the man sounded nervous. Heat couldn't remember the last time Vine had really worried about anything. Fielding was on the line as well and he offered up a report, telling them about incoming Tol'An forces and the reinforcements that probably wouldn't get there in time to help.

"Sounds tough," Fielding said. "Chances are good the Tol'An can't get the Orb out of there before you and the Pahxin sweep in and crush them. I'd recommend you wait for the backup and go in with a larger force. Wipe them out *then* bring home the prize. It's the best guarantee we've got."

"Begging your pardon, sir," Heat replied, "but I'm pretty sure the Tol'An are too wily for that. If Vine's right and they're about to blow the wall, they'll be hauling that thing out of here like a bunch of rioters in a smash and grab. At the very least, we have to lock them down so they can't move with it. And that means engaging."

"I think it sounds too dangerous," Fielding said. "You don't even have your full unit."

Heat grunted. "We won't need it. The shaft we're going to is pretty wide open, but the entrance isn't. We can post there and take shots at them. Vine, find out if there's another way out of there that these assholes can use to escape. If not, we've got them. If so, then we'd better plan on rushing in there and wiping them out fast."

Fielding was silent for a time. When he spoke, he began with a sigh. "I'll contact the Pahxin and see if I can get a no bullshit estimate on when they can be there. Maybe we can have them hustle. I don't like it, Heat but do what you have to do down there. You've got more experience with these terrorist assholes than I do."

Heat privately thanked whatever God was out there that the Lieutenant saw things his way. If he hadn't ... Well, they would've had words when the marines returned to the Gnosis. One way or another, Heat was going into that mine shaft and taking on whatever enemies they found.

If that meant disobeying orders, in this case, he was willing to take that chance.

"When we get there," Heat explained, "I want two people taking cover near the entrance. The rest of us will charge in. Vine, what's in there that we can use for cover, anyway? Can you pipe the feed down to us?"

"With all this interference," Vine replied, "I doubt it ... but there's plenty of heavy machinery you can use. You'll see when you get there. If the Tol'An get there first though ... That's going to be a rough space to hold, Gunny. Lots of firepower being tossed around in there and don't forget, it might not be structurally sound."

"You're a total ray of sunshine, Vine," Gillet said. "I'll remember that when we're back on the ship and give you a God damn hug. Pretty clear your mamma never bothered."

"That's enough." Heat waved a hand at Gillet. The ceiling transitioned from manmade metal to natural rock. Another twenty feet, the walls did the same. Two forms seemed to be lying on the ground up ahead. He lifted his weapon, casting a wary eye about the area. "Contact … Sort of."

Gillet stepped forward to investigate. "They're dead. Looks like a knife. They're armed, too so someone managed to get real close first."

"The Tol'An prick that Cassie was talking about," Heat said. "Wearing a Kalrawv uniform. I bet his new buddies don't know he did this. Move out."

They moved into the tunnel, leaving behind the metal floor for rock. Heat's HUD showed there was plenty of oxygen down there, that some kind of environmental control system was in full effect. Temperature showed a little on the high side as it pushed eighty degrees Fahrenheit which probably made the miners pretty miserable once they really got going for the day.

Scans indicated they were approaching life forms, several of them. Kalrawv or Tol'An? They didn't hear any violence so he doubted the latter had shown up yet. Once the imposter had his own people to boss around, he wouldn't need anyone else. Of course, they were about to blow up a wall for him.

Maybe he hoped they wouldn't survive the blast.

"We're about to enter the main area," Heat said. "Check your targets in case there are—"

An explosion shook the floor, making dust fall from the ceiling. The marines around Heat held their weapons up, each ready to start shooting. "We're not being shelled," he said. "That was them blowing the wall. If the Orb's behind it, they probably see it right now. Let's make this quick while they're distracted by the pretty."

Heat picked up the pace, dashing forward. His HUD showed an influx of new targets, additional life forms in the larger room ahead. *Great, his buddies made it.* The maintenance tunnel they used likely wouldn't have worked for the marines considering their armor, but a light unit probably made a quick run of it.

That's how they were already there and that's why Heat and his crew were about to have their hands full. Even as he knew they didn't have time, half of him wanted to wait for his own reinforcements. Fielding was right that it would be the smart thing to do but maybe not the best course of action considering the severity of the situation.

At least the Tol'An don't have those sonic weapons. That'll be a small favor.

Shouting filled the air, then the wheezing of the sonic weapons. Familiar beam weapons discharged, the Tol'An taking shots. Heat rushed ahead, reaching the larger room and moving in without pause, taking cover behind a massive drill. The few steps between the opening and that safety revealed a wild display of chaotic violence.

Tol'An soldiers, dressed in their black jump suits stood their ground while blasted away at the Kalrawv security forces, who ran for cover. Gillet called out to him, asking for target prioritization. He struggled with the question. There were more Tol'An but their weapons weren't as nasty.

"Targets of opportunity," Heat shouted. "If you've got a shot, take it. I don't care who it is out there. Wrap this up!"

Their projectile weapons added to the clatter, guns popping as the marines engaged. Heat leaned out and fired some quick bursts, tearing through a Tol'An who stood in the open as if he were immune to weapon fire.

A couple more went down, torn up by both the Kalrawv agents and other marines. The combined firepower finally drove them to take some cover of their own as their superior numbers were whittled down. Another couple of explosions went off, smaller than the first. Heat put his money on grenades but couldn't see from his vantage.

As before, dust fell from the ceiling, this time with chunks of rock accompanying it. Heat's HUD offered a warning about structural integrity, then gave him a reading on how many tons of ground happened to be suspended above them. *Not the time!* Heat darted from behind cover again, taking another couple of shots.

Two of the yellow beams whizzed by him and he had to hit the dirt to avoid being caught by them. Kalrawv tried to take back the initiative, shouting to one another as they laid into the two forces with their superior weapons.

Heat risked a glance toward the wall. It had opened up into a metal chamber, not at all the rock formation surrounding them. Five guys were rolling the Orb out, moving toward a tall passage to the left. *That must be there for all this heavy equipment. It probably has a straight shot to some kind of docking bay too.*

The fight continued but those five guys, and probably Gizan, all made their way out of the conflict.

"We don't have time for this!" Heat shouted. "We need to get after those guys! They've got the Orb!"

"Kinda pinned down over here!" Gillet shouted.

"I can't go either!" Bosh called as well. "We've gotta secure this room first!"

"Damn it." Heat considered his options. The other sounded off that they were in a bad place to go for it. He looked to his right, noting he had the larger machine providing cover to the wall. He *might* be able to make it but then, he'd be facing five on his own. *I don't mind those odds.* "Gillet, I'm going for it."

"Gunny, are you nuts?"

"I have pretty decent cover all the way to their exit point. I'll at least try to slow them down while the rest of you clear up this rabble." Heat rolled back toward his cover and rose, pausing at the edge. He was about to dart out. "Hey, catch up as soon as you can, huh? I like your company."

Heat dashed out and ran beside the wall. He made it ten paces before energy beams slapped the wall over his head, showering him with pebbles. Another ten paces got him to another machine and cover from the Tol'An. A Kalrawv security soldier turned and stared at him, spinning his weapon around to take a shot.

Heat already had the initiative and blasted him center mass with two three round bursts. The body collapsed backward and someone shouted just as Heat started running again.

Another soldier appeared in front of him and he threw his arm out, clotheslining him in the chin with all the enhanced strength the power armor afforded. Heat didn't even feel the collapse of the man's bones, but he knew it happened. He also couldn't risk taking a look behind him as he was nearly to his destination.

Two Tol'An stood guard at the passage and they started firing as Heat approached. The first energy blast struck his torso armor, which absorbed it completely. Another hit his shoulder but a third missed.

Heat returned fire, catching one in the head and the other in the stomach chest. The first died immediately but the other wore a shield. He dropped to the ground but remained alive, struggling to regain his footing. Before he could, Heat charged up and kicked him in the face.

The shield couldn't protect him against that and his head caved in. Heat made it to the passage and charged in, hoping he wasn't too late. "I'm in guys," he announced. "Sooner you can get here the better." He saved the rest of his breath for the fight to come. It promised to be one of the more nasty ones he'd ever been in.

***

Micah sensed when the bombs hit the destroyer before anything else. A part of him knew they'd gone off, some extrasensory perception he only had due to rampaging adrenaline. The concussive force of all that ordnance tore through the enemy's defenses, but it wasn't enough to obliterate it entirely.

Those were some solid shields.

The enemy ship charged the Gnosis, moving toward them at ramming speed. *Oh God.* Micah's heart raced, and he craned his neck to see. Flames burst from where they'd been struck, and the engines flickered but still managed to compel them forward at an alarming speed.

There's no way they're going to catch the Gnosis ... But Micah couldn't put much conviction behind the thought. He was shocked to see his home ship practically spin on a dime and burst away at top speed. *Zach knows how to handle that bus like a real pro. God, I don't envy him right now.*

Micah's computer started buzzing, indicating he'd made it to the minimal safe distance. He didn't slow down, allowing the engines to remain in the redline for a little longer. Still, his attention remained fixed on the destroyer as it chased the Gnosis, like some kind of rampaging demon out of a horror movie.

When it finally couldn't go on anymore, the reactor went critical, shattering the vessel like a piece of porcelain. One moment, it was a flaming behemoth, the next, merely an empty space where only embers remained. But even as it disappeared from existence, seemingly with all hands, the aftermath battered the Gnosis from behind.

Micah watched the shields flare and wink out. Various bits sparked over the surface of the hull before going dark. Thrusters shut down and the ship seemed to drift, lumbering away from the force of being shoved by the explosion. He held his breath, wondering if they had been destroyed or somehow finished off.

Half a moment later, the engines came to life but only the environmental shields lit up. Someone was alive, at the very least, and the ship itself survived. He looked forward to docking, to help out with whatever needed to happen for the return trip. But first, he tuned into the search and rescue com channel, patching it in for the others.

"This is Rhino Two. Our squadron is available to assist with pick up efforts. Please direct us and we'll do what we can."

"Glad to hear from you," Commander Bowman replied. His voice was mired in static, but he was still legible. "We have a number of downed ships out there that need some help. I'm sending you coordinates."

"Got it." Micah cleared his throat. "How's Nolan? Did he make it?"

"Just," Bowman said. "Right before the destroyer went off, he landed. When things settle down, he's heading to sick bay but right now, he's helping secure the hangar for everyone coming back. Hey ... I wanted to tell you ... thanks. You did great work out there. It was you that finished it off. Thank you."

"No problem ... and I'm glad to hear he's okay." Micah grinned. "You guys hear that?"

"Thank you, sir," Mariah added. "That was ... intense. Can you believe they blew their own reactor?"

"I'm going to let you guys get to it. If you need anything, speak up. The com's a little crowded right now, though so keep it to a minimum on the open. Bowman out."

"I can believe it," Deanne added as the Commander dropped off. "They've proven they don't have any sort of real self-preservation to speak of. The last time we met these creeps, remember?"

"Well, we do," Micah added. "And now, let's prove it by finding our people. Come on. Looks like Mustang One's first on the list. Area's still a little hot but we've got quite a bit of firepower between us, so we'll carve a perimeter and get these folks back. We'll be there long before the shuttles. Let's put the time to good use."

***

Gizan ordered the duped Kalrawv men to blow the wall. The detonation would go off before his people arrived, but they'd be there soon. Just in time to help remove the Trindisha. They had a direct line to the surface from the maintenance tunnels, a bit he picked up from downloading the schematics.

His Kalrawv lackeys gawked at their find, eyes wide. The officer probably knew what it was, but he played ignorant. Gizan smiled, still playing the role. "Behold why we're here. The power to elevate our company to new heights. I suppose you're all glad you listened to me now, eh?"

One of them shouted, gesturing as the Tol'An men poured into the room. Gizan quickly tore off the top of his uniform so he wouldn't be killed by friendly fire. A firefight broke out, driving him to cover. He gestured wildly at several of his men, ordering them to advance on his position.

Kalrawv weapons tore some of them down but when Gizan fired into their backs, they were forced to seek their own cover. That bought time for five Tol'An to arrive and they dislodged the Trindisha from its home. It appeared to be some forgotten room, a space used by the previous people who had lived there before.

Human weapons went off, barking off the ceiling. Gizan cursed. Their soldiers were not as easily beaten back as the Kalrawv dogs were. He needed to move quickly if he hoped to get his prize to the ship.

"Act as if your lives depend on this!" Gizan shouted. "Because I assure you it is true. If this is not on the ship before we leave, you will all die. Me too, likely. Now … go! Hurry!"

They hoisted it out, kicking the fragile rocks out of the way before rolling it into the open area. Gizan didn't bother to request they be careful. He knew the thing was tough but even if it wasn't, they didn't have the luxury of time. Five men shoved it toward the opening, which appeared to be just about right to get the Trindisha through it.

I'm glad these fools have multiple avenues to bring in their mining toys. Gizan drove his people on, shouting at them to hurry. The battle raged around them and the echoes of shouts and weapon fire made it so he had to scream at the top of his lungs to be heard over the clamor.

Once they were in the tunnel, the sound deadened somewhat but they were hampered by moving uphill. Gizan threw himself against the Trindisha, helping them shove it up the hill. The combined strength of all of them made decent time. He wasn't entirely sure how far they had to go but providing his people kept the other soldiers busy, it wouldn't matter.

They took a right as the incline increased. Light up ahead indicated they were approaching outside. A loading dock sat there and one of the Tol'An shuttles waited. Gizan felt the thrill of success teasing the back of his neck, spurring him on. If he wanted, he would be back in the good grace of Ezria.

Succeeding meant making difficult choices, it meant deciding what to do with the rest of his life. One thing he absolutely vowed was to ensure they remained in *his* hands alone. That was the important part. No more would he be the puppet of another, allowing his fate to teeter on another's whim.

Especially not a man like Ezria, who quite easily and readily killed his own people for minor infractions. The men around him knew what their leader was like. Some of them may have even lost friends to his mercurial attitude. When Gizan returned the Trindisha, he felt it may be time to part ways with the Tol'An for good.

A shout behind them gave him pause. The other men continued shoving. He turned, cocking his head as he listened to the heavy footfalls of a human marine. *That blasted armor!* He cursed. *How did this fool get through the others? The Kalrawv? Our own people? He must have an absolute death wish!*

Gizan drew the sonic weapon from his belt and considered how to proceed. If he missed, the man would likely kill him with ease. Perhaps that wasn't necessary. Suppressing him may be enough to buy his people some time. They didn't need much. Once the Trindisha was on board, they could flee the system.

Victory would be theirs.

But where does that leave me? Gizan really questioned that. He already determined he wanted to leave the Tol'An behind. Was it worth risking his life in that moment to preserve their victory? Honor suggested he fulfill his obligation.

Regardless of his future, he committed to the present and that meant success.

What would the Tol'An do with another Trindisha? Ezria didn't care about the wondrous technology that could come from the devices. He wanted power sources, information about his enemy's whereabouts and ultimately, the ability to control the universe. What others did with them didn't have any bearing on the man's plans.

It was a far cry from the way things worked before.

Gizan shook his head. "No," he muttered. "I will not betray the Tol'An today. I may never return, but I will do my duty today."

He saw the marine making his way up the incline. Taking aim, Gizan fired twice, the wheezing gun discharging two yellow beams that raced toward his target. The marine hit the ground the instant he pulled the trigger, avoiding both attacks while returning fire.

Gizan dove for cover. One of his own people cried out in pain. A glance back showed he'd taken three bullets to the back, right in the spine. The damage caused him to hit the floor, screaming in agony. His fellows didn't even look down at him as they continued shoving the Trindisha toward its destination.

"You're only one man!" Gizan shouted from the tiny cover of a protruding rock. "You should just go back the other way. You've lost this round. We have the Trindisha. Save your life for another battle, human!"

"Not how we operate," the marine yelled back. "Pahxin forces are locking the facility down. We've got air superiority. Do you really think you're getting off the planet with that thing? Just leave it there and I'm sure you can escape with your lives. We'll be too busy securing the Orb."

"That's right, you have a colloquial name for what you don't understand." Gizan sneered. "I stand here ready to kill you, human. I've got one of the Kalrawv weapons. Your precious little armor you encase yourself in won't protect you. Besides, how much longer will you allow yourself to be delayed? My people are succeeding."

"Maybe," the marine replied, "but I've still got one of these. Might put a damper on your ... success."

Gizan risked a glance. He didn't know what was happening to the man's back but something on the armor was moving. *Is the fool going to blow the power core on that thing? It could destroy the entire tunnel!* He turned and began to run, dashing toward the exit. A sudden hiss filled the air and he risked another look.

A projectile raced along the passage, not necessarily toward Gizan but certainly in his direction. A gray-white stream of smoke erupted from the back of it, leaving behind a mist in its wake.

He dove to the floor, landing hard enough for the stone to dig into his elbows, forearms and knees. Pain danced through his nerves, but he shrugged it off while tilting his head just in time to see the thing fly over him. It struck the mouth of the cavern near the men with the Trindisha, exploding in a spectacular bright flash.

Chunks of the wall collapsed, crushing one of Gizan's men and rolling over another's leg. They were immobilized, temporarily trapped by the attack. If the ship was ready, there'd be other men who could help dislodge it but not before they had to contend with additional troops barreling down on their position.

Gizan turned to look at the marine who had reclaimed his feet and began to advance. The Trindisha no longer concerned him nearly as much as surviving the next few moments. As he scrambled for his weapon, he realized he'd dropped it when he fell. Armed with only a knife, he needed to make a choice on how to proceed: flee and live or risk death by staying.

***

Gillet tapped his jump jets, aiming himself to the left. His body was thrown toward cover and he landed hard, rolling several times until he came to a halt against the wall. Tol'An forces kept coming from the wall, as if they had a never-ending supply. The Kalrawv operatives stopped firing, electing to cower in the relative safety of their positions.

The other marines popped off shots, maintaining their mobility throughout the fight. They darted between different bits of cover, but they were taking some serious damage. He hadn't been able to take a census, but at least two men had gone down, possibly dead. Regardless of their defenses or the number they killed, the odds were stacked against them.

An energy blast hit Gillet's left arm, spinning him in place. He hit the ground, leaning against one of the large pieces of machinery. His HUD showed minimal damage, but his shoulder hurt like hell. *Probably dislocated, at least a little bit.* He tried to move it and winced. *Yeah, this is the problem with wearing the armor: it's not so easy to shove back in.*

"Human marine units," a soft voice spoke in his helmet. "This is Finda of the Stalwart. We are coming upon your rear. Please check your fire as we are here to reinforce you. Please respond."

"About time!" Gillet shouted. "Watch your fire to the six, guys!" Despite the hope he felt filling his chest, he still aimed his weapon down the hall back toward where their supposed allies were coming. If they were lying, if they somehow managed to break the coms and were enemies, he didn't want to be shot in the back.

Blaster fire tore at his cover, chipping it away as chunks of metal were thrown clear. As Gillet looked around, he noted the other marines were in similar situations. If they tried to move, they'd likely be tagged. It was a nasty situation that would've required rockets to even the odds.

Unfortunately, the roof didn't seem to be structurally sound, at least not enough to take a couple more explosions. The Tol'An had already saw to that.

The first of the Pahxin men dashed inside, wearing their blue uniforms. When they started shooting at the Tol'An, Gillet finally let himself believe they'd been saved. He gave them a moment to pour in, nearly twenty of them right away, before he ordered the marines to get up and help.

Concentrated fire drove the Tol'An back toward the maintenance tunnel they'd entered from, which kept them away from Heat. Several Pahxin dashed after them, running headlong into the corridor with their weapons at the ready. The firefight continued in there while other Pahxin secured prisoners of the Kalrawv people.

Another explosion sounded down the hallway and Gillet scowled. *God damn it!* Was it the Tol'An again or had Heat done something crazy? Before he could ask, Heat's voice filled his helmet. "Listen up, I need the transport shuttle to come down to my position. There may be Tol'An ships in the area but this is an urgent request for evac."

Establishing your coordinates now." The response came from some pilot, but the words were so colored in static it was impossible to make out which one.

"Heat?" Gillet asked. "You're still alive up there! What the hell was that explosion? Are you okay?"

Chapter 11

Heat watched the rocket fly, bringing down massive chunks of wall onto the retreating Tol'An. He recognized the gamble, knew it could've ended badly but he didn't have a lot of options. Time, as always, worked directly against him. Inaction would've cost him the Orb, just as action almost did the same.

Heat got to his feet and began to advance. "Connect to tactical com." The words made his armor comply. It only took a moment before a green light on his HUD showed he would be heard. "Listen up, I need the transport shuttle to come down to my position. There may be Tol'An ships in the area, but this is an urgent request for evac."

"Establishing your coordinates now." A static filled response made him wince. He didn't even know who spoke.

"Heat?" Gillet asked. "You still alive up there? What the hell was that explosion? Are you okay?"

"I'm fine," Heat replied. "But if you're available, I could sure use some backup right about now."

"Pahxin got here and helped us out. We'll be right there."

Heat breathed a sigh of relief. The man who spoke earlier seemed to be gone. Only three of the five Tol'An who worked on the Orb were still alive, but they'd managed to get the device outside. Heat took aim and fired, grazing one on the shoulder just as they moved left beyond his view.

Damn it! Heat picked up the pace, racing after them. He reached the opening and slowed down, risking a quick peek. A Tol'An ship sat on a docking pad just two hundred yards away. Several men were running toward the Orb, their weapons hanging from their shoulders as they moved.

Heat considered what to do. If he fired in a way that might suppress the men out there, he'd undoubtedly hit the Orb. He had no idea how volatile the thing was. No one ever tried to shoot them back on Earth, not as far as he knew. Cassie and Thayne talked about them being power sources and that meant it could probably blow up.

I have to be cautious. Heat thought about that and realized maybe being careful was the exact wrong thing to do. He checked his HUD, noting the wind was a lot calmer on that side of the facility than it had been when they arrived. It might still be dangerous, but he could put himself in the way of their escape. *God, I hope this is a good idea.*

Heat stepped outside and hit the jump pack, flying high into the air. He didn't clear the stone wall to his left, it towered another hundred feet above him. The wind slapped at him, but he was able to use maneuvering bursts from his thrusters, keeping him from veering too far off course.

He sailed over the Orb and managed to land in front of the walkway leading to the Tol'An cargo ship. The other soldiers had just cleared it and were moving toward the Orb when they spun in place. *Well, shit.* Heat took aim and started firing, blasting into their ranks. He still had to take care not to get the Orb but at least there were more targets to catch his rounds.

The sky opened up, pouring rain down upon the area. Drops slapped Heat's helmet, causing tiny beads to rush across his vision. He put himself in motion, turning into a moving target as he laid into the crowd. They did the same, darting toward him and moving to the left and right.

Three of them went down in his first pass but he paid for his victory. A shot caught his leg and another nailed him in the torso, just below the chest. He used the jump pack again, this time to buy him a moment of relief from the constant barrage of energy beams.

When Heat came down a good twenty feet away, he nearly toppled off the walkway to the ground below. The ground looked small from his height, but the worst part was the fact that he didn't have anywhere else to move. Another jump was the only way to evade and as the Tol'An took aim to fire again, he had to risk it.

The storm intensified. Thunder accompanied the downpour. Lightning lanced through the sky. Close by, a sound of engines rumbled, echoing off the rocks. Heat launched himself again, this time moving toward the docked Tol'An vessel. He landed just in front of their ramp, tossing a grenade inside.

A shout inside threw some men into action. One of them darted out just as it went off. Heat blasted the man before he made it two feet and shoved his body to the side, darting onto the space craft.

Heat found himself in a cargo bay, only barely large enough to get the Orb on board. A hallway led off toward the cockpit and he saw some chairs facing one another along the way. His grenade killed one, incapacitated another but down the hall, others had managed to escape the worst of it.

He fell back so he wasn't standing in the door and opened up on the mouth of the hallway, suppressing the others from coming into the room. Injuries began to catch up with him, pain from being shot in multiple locations. The armor held, but the concussion went right through somehow.

"I'm on the enemy ship," Heat announced to his com. "I'll try to keep them from boarding, but I can't make any promises right now. This ... was probably my craziest idea to date."

"You think?" Gillet asked. "We're about to come outside now. Pahxin are with us and one of our ships is almost to the scene. They *were* going to blast the Tol'An ship, man. We can't now that you're on board."

"Sorry," Heat replied, "there wasn't a lot of choice for me out there alone."

Gunfire erupted outside as the marines closed on the enemy flank. A couple energy beams burst through the hallway, slapping the wall to Heat's left. He returned fire until his magazine was spent. Dropping the mag, he leaned into the wall. Anyone trying to hit him would have to commit to leaning out.

Heat slapped another magazine into his weapon and took aim, forcing himself to be patient. Finally, one of the Tol'An popped his head out and Heat's finger squeezed the trigger, killing the target in an instant. He waited for another when a blast to his right drew his attention to the door.

Cursing, he felt the blast before he could even look. It hit him right in the side just below the ribs, pressing him into the wall before he lost his footing and slid to the ground. Another blast caught him in the chest and pain welled up through his senses, making his vision go white. He coughed, struggling to lift his weapon.

I guess this is it. The thought danced through Heat's mind, giving him a sense of acceptance. The Tol'An advanced on him, their weapons at the ready. At any moment, they would open up, ending the battle. *Here I come, Gorman. I guess you couldn't be alone for long after all.*

***

Gillet and his men burst out onto the walk, opening up on the Tol'An surrounding the Orb. They abandoned the device, darting about for cover that wasn't there. One of them fell off the landing, tumbling down hundreds of feet to a messy death.

As suddenly as they had started dashing about, they charged the marines and Pahxin, shouting in defiance. They were cut down in a few moments, torn apart by concentrated fire from well over twenty weapons. A couple stray rounds got through, but Gillet's people finished that fight in a hurry.

More blasts went off nearby and he saw several Tol'An darting toward the shuttle. Rain battered him from all sides, but he risked a jump anyway, throwing himself over to the ramp leading aboard the vessel. When he landed with a massive clatter, one of the Tol'An spun just in time to see the brief muzzle flashes of Gillet's rifle before being cut down.

The others turned but Gillet kept shooting, finishing them off in quick succession.

More marines joined him as the Pahxin secured the Orb. Gillet led them on board. Heat was collapsed in the corner, his armor scorched and blackened from energy beams. "Check on him," he gestured. "Get him out of here. We don't have to clear this thing. Just keep your weapons aimed so they don't come out."

Two marines collected Heat and dragged him off the ship. Gillet was the last one to depart, stepping backward down the ramp so he could keep his weapon trained on the hallway. None of the enemy seemed to be willing to peek out. When the ramp started to lift, he understood why.

They intended to flee.

"The Tol'An shuttle is departing," Gillet said over the com. "They do *not* have the Orb. I repeat, the Orb is in our possession."

"That's great news," Fielding replied, though his message was garbled pretty bad. "Sounds like we've got this one in the bag right now, gentleman. Where's the Gunny?"

"I'm checking on him now." Gillet stepped over to Heat and crouched beside him and Bosh. "How's he doing?"

"He's hurt," Bosh replied, "but okay. His com's messed up though. Looks like his armor took a real pounding."

The shuttle launched beside them, rocketing away from the area. Their own took its place a moment later, landing with a metallic thump that echoed off the rocks. "Let's get him on board. He goes back with the Orb." Gillet turned to the Pahxin. "If you need to get anyone to a medical bay, this is going straight back to the Gnosis."

Wounded were gathered and deposited on the shuttle. Gillet paced away, looking over the carnage of dead bodies and damage done by the battle. He shook his head, wondering how many people died during the operation. He knew they had lost some of their own. It had been a bloody situation.

Heat's voice crackled in his speakers just after the ramp closed to the shuttle. "Hey," he muttered. "The Tol'An guy Cassie talked about … He got away."

"Slippery son of a bitch," Gillet muttered. "We'll look for him. Are you okay? What the hell happened?"

"I got shot … a lot. This armor saved my life but that automatic shield thing never kicked in for me. I guess I burned it out doing something else."

"Hang in there, buddy. This getting hurt thing's starting to become a habit."

"Not one I'm happy with," Heat replied. "Make sure Cassie gets back to the ship okay … and that we've really wrapped up down here. You're in charge. Don't let me down."

"You just relax and worry about feeling better," Gillet said. "I'll see you back on the ship." He turned to the others. "We're going back to the control room to grab Agent Alexander before we leave this planet. Fall in behind me, folks. There's still a dangerous animal running around this base and we can't afford to let our guard down now."

***

Ulian's heart thumped hard in his chest as the Tol'An vessels disengaged the Kalrawv battleship and started to flee the scene. The only reason they would be leaving is if they finished their objective, if they found their prize. His mind raced as he tried to decide what to do, and how to slow them down.

But it was evident that the vessels near to his ship wouldn't have the Trindisha on them. They were there to distract the military forces while the smaller ships went to the surface. They hadn't been able to harass them enough to prevent their landing and now, they seemed to have succeeded.

The final Kalrawv destroyer was destroyed, leaving only the battleship standing between them and a decisive military victory. Morala had proven herself capable of leading such an attack, albeit in a brusque manner. They would've walked away with a complete victory if the humans had been able to secure their target.

I cannot believe that Captain Bradford's people would have failed.

"Engaging final target," Morala said. "Erda, target their aft section, thirty meters from the thrusters. Concentrate all fire on that point."

"Ma'am?" Erda asked.

"I noticed the Tol'An were pounding that area pretty hard," Morala explained. "The defenses should be weakened there."

The battleship wasted no time in redirecting their own efforts, firing on the Stalwart as soon as they were no longer being harassed by the Tol'An. A number of energy blasts struck the ship, causing it to shake violently. When they stabilized, Erda shot back, launching everything they had at the targeted area.

Ulian watched the view screen, brow furrowed in a grim expression. Their beams caught the hull of their target, popping holes in two sections. Fire popped out for only a moment before emergency shields sealed the breach, but it would only be a matter of time before they were destroyed with that kind of damage.

"You were right, ma'am!" Erda shouted. "I'm powering up for another volley."

"Damage report," Morala said. "How bad did their attack hurt us?"

"Major damage to cargo bay two," Viran said, "not a breach but all electronics are down … including gravity. Two crewmen were in there … it sounds like they might be …" She sighed. "Minor damage to crew decks six and seven. Observation deck has also been brought offline."

"Non-essentials, one and all," Morala muttered. "Good. They didn't bother to target us, they just shot blindly and hoped. Return fire, Erda. Knock them out of the sky."

"Belay that order," Ulian said, stepping in. "Viran, raise the enemy ship and offer them terms."

Morala shot a look at him. "Sir, begging your pardon, but the Kalrawv Group are well known for *never* surrendering."

"And that will likely hold true here," Ulian replied. "We have the upper hand, we're going to make the offer. Remember, we can always destroy a ship but you can't offer it mercy when it's gone."

Viran got on the com and reached out to the enemy vessel. Her calm voice offered them terms for surrender. After she finished, Erda cried out, slapping his console with several rapid taps. The ship lurched downward, nearly stealing Ulian's breath before it stopped. Just as suddenly, they darted to the side, jostling everyone about.

"What happened?" Morala asked.

"Evasive maneuvers," Erda said. "They fired again."

Ulian shook his head. "Proceed, Morala." He clenched his fist, frustrated by their decision. *They are throwing away so many lives. What policy does that organization have that pushes people to the brink of death rather than survival? We must look into it and stop this practice. The waste ... is disgusting.*

Morala gave the order to fire and Erda followed throw, casting another volley in their opponent's direction. The battleship began to roll, fire billowing from the same surgical place they hit before. It might not have been enough to destroy their ship, but it took them out of the fight, at least temporarily.

"Fighters," Morala said, "report. Have you mopped up the enemy forces?"

"The few that were left have fled," came the reply. "We are initiating search and rescue at this time."

Morala grinned, turning to Ulian. "I'd call this a decisive victory, would you not?"

Ulian nodded, still too ill with the decision of the Kalrawv to take much pleasure in the win. He'd completed several combat missions, most successfully but until he faced the Tol'An and these corporate mercenaries, his opponents always showed reasonable judgement. They offered quarter where it was necessary and surrendered when they could not win.

This new enemy disgusted him.

"Finish them off, Erda," Morala said, "they're likely going to blow their reactor. Don't give them the chance."

Ulian turned to his reports as the battleship was annihilated. All those lives, men and women, some of which weren't even full-time employees of the corporation, were lost. If the Tol'An escaped with the Trindisha, then it was all for nothing. Every person dead would be chalked up to an overall failure.

Much as Morala wanted to take credit for a combat victory, it would be nothing if the true objective flew away.

He contacted the Gnosis to find out their status and discover what happened on the surface. Hopefully, they had some positive news, something to make up for the resources spent on their errand. He didn't look forward to explaining what happened to his superiors if they weren't bringing home the prize.

It would be the only justification for attacking the Kalrawv Group as they had.

***

Vincent smiled as he turned to Desmond, patting the captain on the shoulder. It drew an annoyed look. "I just heard from the marines," he spoke quietly. "They secured the Orb and it's on the way backup here right now!"

Desmond slumped in his seat. "That's wonderful news. Thank God that worked out." He turned to Salina. "Reach out to the Stalwart so we can give them the good news." Looking back at Vincent, he asked, "what about Cassie and the others? Do we have any casualty reports yet?"

Vincent sobered and turned away. "Not yet. The marines sent the ship back up with the wounded and the Orb. They'll return soon but Fielding didn't tell me what they're doing. He was trying to coordinate something. I'll reach back out to him shortly. The bombers are on search and rescue. Our fighters are coming back home."

"Good." Desmond rubbed his eyes. "Has engineering given us an estimated time for when we can get out of here?"

"They're working on it," Salina said. "They're working on required systems only. Anything else will be bonus at this point."

Vincent tried to reach out to Cassie, sending a message to the surface. He cursed under his breath when the interference once again prevented it. *How the hell is Fielding talking to them?* He reached out to the lieutenant. "How can I speak to the people down there? Are you still able to?"

"There's a massive electrical storm, sir," Fielding replied. "That's why we can't reach the surface. It should pass in the next fifteen minutes. Then, we'll be back in business."

Fifteen minutes is a lifetime in a hostile environment. Vincent sighed. "Understood. Thank you for that."

"Salina," Desmond said, "get Ulian on screen. Let's ease his mind a little."

"They're reaching out to us right now," Salina replied. "I'll put them on."

Ulian appeared on the screen, brow furrowed. "Captain Bradford," he spoke in a solemn tone of voice. "The Tol'An forces fled the system. Do you know if they were successful in taking the Trindisha? Do we need to attempt a pursuit?"

Desmond shook his head. "We don't. Our boys have the Orb and are bringing it back to the Gnosis now."

Shock widened Ulian's eyes. "Why...why would they have left then? That makes no sense."

"I'll chalk it up to good fortune for us," Desmond replied. "We're wrapping up over here. How're things your way?"

"The same. The enemy forces are neutralized ... our pilots are collecting those who had to eject." Ulian shrugged. "We need to conduct some repairs before we can go. What about those on the surface? We are not able to raise our soldiers there. The interference on that planet is incredible."

"Same for us," Desmond replied. "We did hear from them shortly before the electrical storm kicked in and that's how we know about the Orb. They're collecting the remainder of our people and they'll be on their way back. We have some repairs to do ourselves. No estimate on how long we'll need. Do you think the area is safe?"

"We'll form a perimeter," Ulian said. "And do whatever it takes to remain so until we can leave this system. We will be safe enough, Captain. Ulian out."

Vincent turned away from the interaction and started worrying about the people still on the surface. He couldn't even pretend it wasn't mostly about Cassie and that's why he didn't voice his concerns out loud. Desmond already knew his judgement wasn't entirely clear when it came to the Agent.

The fact she went down there at all bothered Vincent more than it should have. She was capable but after what had just happened to her, it seemed like an unnecessary risk. Still, she had managed to fix communications and God knows how useful she was on the surface. He would've rather her been on the bridge, helping them there.

I have to find a way to be okay with this. Though he wondered how long he had to worry about it. Once the Tol'An was defeated, the fighting would essentially end. There would be no war, no terrorist organization flying around causing trouble. Perhaps humanity could get on with the research and exploration they hoped for.

But until then, Cassie would not be leaving the Gnosis for the relative safety of Gamma Alpha and Vincent needed to come to terms with it. He busied himself with reports from various sections of the ship, focusing on helping department heads with their problems. It distracted him from his worries, but they remained, in the back of his mind.

And likely would until Cassie was back on the ship.

***

"Damn it!" Cassie slapped the side of the monitor out of frustration, drawing a wide-eyed look from Jayla. She sighed. "Sorry ... I'm tired of all this interference. We can't get through to the ship through that electrical storm. No matter what I've tried, tight beam, blasting it ... Nothing's working."

"Gillet just talked to me," Vine said. "They sent the Orb up to the Gnosis."

"Did they leave us here?" Cassie asked.

Vine chuckled. "No, they're on their way to us now." He paused. "Oh."

"What is it?" Jayla asked. "What's the matter?"

"Um ... one of the Tol'An guys ... the one you talked about ... Seems he got away."

"No!" Jayla paced away from the terminal. "He was a mad man! A violent criminal!"

Cassie moved over and touched the woman's shoulder. "Relax. We're not going to let him do anything to you, Jayla. You're safe with us."

"Am I?" Jayla shook away, backing into the wall. "You people attacked this facility without provocation. And for what?"

"A Trindisha," Cassie said. "Kalrawv came for it and that's why we had to come. We'll take you with us and get you out of here. From what I understand of this ... company ... they blame anyone they can for a failure. I don't think you want to be here when they come around looking for that scapegoat."

A wheezing shot sounded from one of the doorways. Vine cried out, falling to the floor in an instant. Cassie lifted her rifle and aimed it as Gizan stepped into the room, pointing the Kalrawv pistol in her general direction. She swore she would tremble in his presence but instead, a severe calm fell over her, a profound state of focus.

Jayla, on the other hand, freaked out and fell to the floor. She started crying, covering her face.

"I see she hasn't changed," Gizan spat. "You're with the human vessel ... the Gnosis."

Cassie nodded once but didn't speak.

"My people left me. It seems you've won. Again." Gizan shook his head. "I would like to understand your skill ... your tenacity. The fact you employ women shows you have the same sort of sickening openness of the Pahxin government. Perhaps that's where the Tol'An have failed. The doctrine requires intolerance."

"Is there a point to any of this?" Cassie asked. "Why did you come back here?"

"I need the control room," Gizan said. "To locate a way off this planet. I'm guessing your other friends will be along soon, so we don't have much time."

"Pull the trigger," Cassie replied. "Find out what happens."

"We're both too smart for that, aren't we?" Gizan scowled. "If I shoot you and you twitch, then I die. That's what's stayed your hand. Your kind seem like quite the war mongers if you don't mind my saying. Absolute killers. You should've seen what your soldiers did to my men."

"Yeah, quite the atrocity on account of your peaceful protest," Cassie sneered, "you disgust me with your attempt to play this out like you're some kind of victim. I recommend you move on. I'm not surrendering this control room and as you said, reinforcements are on the way."

"Perhaps we can come to an agreement." Gizan started to slide toward Cassie and she took a step back, her legs brushing against the computer console. "Allow me to scan the planet and we don't have to conduct any violence at all. We both win at that point, don't you think?"

"Counter offer," Cassie said. "Put the gun down and I'll ensure you get off this planet as a prisoner of the Pahxin. I'll make sure you're treated fairly until you stand trial for all the crimes you've committed. I'm sure it'll take a while for them to figure them all out, so that should buy you some time. How's that sound?"

"Like we're at an impasse." Gizan lunged toward her. Cassie pulled the trigger. Blood burst from high on his shoulder but he didn't even wince, slapping her weapon aside before she could fire again.

Spinning in place, Cassie brought the weapon back around and slammed it into his good shoulder, driving him toward the computer terminal. Again, she tried to aim the gun but Gizan threw his feet up and kicked it from her hands. The sling kept it attached to her shoulder but as it dropped down, the weight made her wince and fall back.

This gave Gizan an opportunity to regain his footing and he attacked again, throwing a blow toward her head.

Cassie ducked, jabbing toward his stomach. Gizan grabbed her wrist and spun her around, pressing her arm against her back. She leaned back, kicking the console to carry them both to the opposite side of the control platform. His back slammed into the metal and his grip loosened, just enough for her to get free.

Lifting her hands defensively, Cassie stepped back and glared into his eyes. The two remained motionless for a long moment.

"You disgusting animal!" Jayla's voice drew their attention to her. She was holding one of the sonic weapons, pointing it at Gizan. "You murdered Dak, you horrible piece of filth! I should kill you where you stand!"

"I doubt you have it in you," Gizan said. "If you do, pull the trigger, you trite little thing. Kill me if you can."

Jayla fired the weapon into the console near him, sending sparks into the air. Cassie winced away, lifting her own gun. The moment she went for it, Gizan hopped the console and rushed for the door. Bullets tapped the wall near him but he escaped, slipping into the base at an alarming rate.

"Are you okay?" Cassie asked Jayla. The woman nodded. "Good." She took a deep breath and turned her attention to Vine. Dropping down beside him, she noted he'd been hit in the shoulder. She used the suit's external scanner to check him and found that he was alive though he'd been severely hurt by the attack.

The armor vibrated so violently, it seemed to shatter his shoulder and several ribs. If he hadn't been in the suit, he certainly would've died.

Heavy footfalls sounded from down the hall, opposite of where Gizan had fled. The marines would be there any second. Cassie didn't know what to do for Vine. He seemed stable and without taking off the armor, she couldn't apply first aid. It might be better to leave him in there until a doctor could help him anyway.

The marines burst into the room, weapons at the ready. Gillet approached Cassie, crouching beside her. "What the hell happen? We heard gunshots ... is he ... is he ..."

"He's hurt," Cassie replied. "But not dead. He's been shot with one of those sonic weapons." She stood up. "We need to get him back to the ship right away."

"What about me?" Jayla squeaked. She'd been crying so hard, her voice was devastated. One of the marines disarmed her. "Please don't shoot!"

"Hold up." Cassie motioned for the marine to back off. "She's okay. She's coming with us."

Gillet pulled her aside. "Is that a good idea?"

"She's an independent contractor with Kalrawv. She doesn't have any loyalty to them." Cassie motioned around. "Does it look like they're coming to save her? We'll be putting her under guard when we get back to the ship. You realize she helped me get you guys the information you needed to get the Orb, right?"

Gillet cursed under his breath. "Move out, people. We have to get Vine back to the ship not to mention it would be great to leave this shit hole behind. Everyone ready?"

They made an indistinct noise amongst themselves and fell into action. Cassie helped Jayla to her feet, wincing at the pain in her shoulder. Gizan really wrenched her arm around when he grabbed her, and it felt like he'd at the very least strained the muscle. *Ice should do the trick*.

Marines picked up Vine and they all started for the hallway leading back to the breach they'd entered from. Gillet led the way and Cassie happily let him. Providing the shuttle waited outside, they'd be back up and safely aboard the Gnosis. As much as she hadn't minded leaving the ship when necessary, this trip became stressful on a different level.

The threats had always been tertiary until the very end. Chance encounters remained possible but unlikely. Gizan attacking her gave the anxiety meaning, meant she wasn't simply being dramatic. As she listened to the whistling wind outside and rain pounded down on the windows, she realized how lucky she was to be alive.

And that made her both thankful … and afraid.

***

Gizan dashed down the hall at a full sprint. His shoulder burned from where he'd been shot, his back aching from when the little woman threw them against the panel. Looking at her did not give him any sense of danger, especially considering his size advantage. Nevertheless, she held her own and even fired the weapon.

That surprised him the most.

Luck came to his aid, saving him from the worst of the damage but then he heard the distant clatter of her reinforcements and he had to go. Worse, he still didn't have an escape. It dawned on him he might be stuck there. Tol'An forces pulled out. Human and Pahxin secured what they cared about and would also be gone soon.

That left Kalrawv stragglers and civilians. Knowing the government, they would likely send aid for those people. Providing the Stalwart moved on, he may be able to join them and simply slip off the planet on his own. He looped around, heading down a flight of stairs then back toward the quarters he'd been assigned upon arrival.

Panicked civilians gathered around the kiosk Gizan started a fight at, each of them questioning what might happen next. He intermingled with them, even accepted aid from a particularly compassionate woman. She applied pressure to his wound and gave him some water.

No soldiers came into the area, no men in power armor or those carrying weapons. People speculated around him about what might happen next. They discussed worries about Kalrawv's reactions to delays. The miners wanted to get paid but they didn't know if the funds would be released.

Some talked about legal action, others expressed they merely had a desire to get home. Gizan fueled the fires in that direction, stating his own desire to leave that place. Many things would change for him as he departed that planet and the civilians around him would be the catalyst.

The Tol'An no longer had his service. Gizan would allow them to believe he died during the operation, he would disappear. One obstacle stood in his way. The two women in the control room saw his face. They may have even had him on a camera. Getting around could be difficult if they were to circulate it, if they cared.

And after he nearly killed them both, they would very likely care.

One problem at a time, Gizan thought, waiting patiently for his rescue. *They'll be dealt with in time.*

Epilogue

Cassie emerged from the shuttle after Heat and Vine were rolled out on stretchers. Medics immediately went to work on them, releasing the safety catches on their armor to get at them. Several others traveled under their own volition, but they followed along, needing various levels of aid.

Her arm hurt but she didn't think she needed to visit the doctors. Vincent rushed over to her and pulled her in a tight embrace, causing her to wince. He didn't notice, and she clung to him for a moment before drawing back.

"Sorry," Cassie muttered. "My arm ... I'll ... I'll tell you about it later."

Jayla was escorted off the ship by the pilots. She nodded to Cassie, mouthing *thank you* as she passed by. They were taking her to some quarters to get cleaned up and checked out by one of the medics. Cassie figured the Pahxin would take her from them, perhaps returning her to their home world.

"Are we going to be able to leave soon?" Cassie asked.

"There's some damage," Vincent replied, "but it won't take long. Engineering just gave us an estimate of three hours. The Stalwart's on the way here now. We're setting up a perimeter so they can conduct some repairs as well. Kalrawv might get here before we're gone so we have to be ready to bolt."

"I guess no one's in the mood for another fight, huh?" Cassie rubbed her eyes with the heels of her hands. Only then did she notice flecks of blood on her shirt sleeves. "Oh … wow."

"Whose is that?"

"I had to shoot someone." Cassie held up her hand to stop him from questioning her. "That's part of the *later* story. I guess the Orb must be here?"

Vincent nodded. "Secure in the lab we had the other two in. Guards are on it now. There's a lot going on up here." He looked around. "Several of our pilots were shot down. Dennis Arden's in the sick bay. He got banged up pretty bad. Lucky for him, nothing broken but he's definitely down for the count for a week or so at the least."

"Vine and Heat both got hurt." Cassie shook her head. "Vine might be better off than Heat. Gillet explained on the way back to the ship how many times the man got shot. He's tough as hell but I think he'd do well to come back from a mission without getting blasted for once."

Vincent smirked but shook his head. "I'll talk to Fielding about instilling some caution in these guys."

"His recklessness might've been what prevented the Tol'An from getting away with the Orb."

"So we'll find a way to gently tell them to be careful." Vincent gestured with his head for her to follow him and they left the hangar. "I'm guessing you'd like to get cleaned up and have something to eat. How about we meet at the mess deck in thirty minutes? I'll buy you free coffee."

"That sounds nice," Cassie said. "Won't the captain want a report? A debriefing?"

"I convinced him we have plenty of time for that during the hyperspace jump." Vincent paused as they got into the hall. "What's the deal with the lady you brought back?"

"Civilian that helped me out. She's okay I think. Witnessed something pretty horrible." Cassie felt grubby. Running a hand through her hair made her sneer. "I'll see you soon. I've got to get this rain or whatever it is out of my hair."

"Take your time." Vincent gripped her good shoulder. "I'll be waiting."

Cassie returned to her quarters and sat at her desk, bringing up the video footage she took of the mission. Down in the mine shaft, when the Stalwart spoke to the imposter, she had a good image of him. Magnifying it, she confirmed it was the man she fought with in the control room.

He was still out there somewhere, and the authorities had to know. She made a copy and set it aside to be deployed with her report. He might've thought he got away, that he'd be able to disappear, but Cassie intended to prove him wrong. Eventually, Gizan would be caught and tried for his actions.

But he wasn't her concern about the moment. Stripping down, she looked at herself in the mirror, sucking air through her teeth when she saw the bruising around her shoulder. Getting cleaned up felt wonderful but once she calmed down, once the adrenaline completely wore off, she was sore all over.

A meal and a nap sounded like just the thing. Providing she'd be allowed to sleep, Cassie figured she'd be mostly recovered in a few hours. Heading to the mess hall, she intended to wind down and let the mission go. There would be time to relive it during her briefing.

***

Ulian acknowledged the damage report and turned his attention to Morala. She stood in front of his desk, in the privacy of his office but her posture was ramrod perfect. Eyes stared straight ahead, like a new recruit waiting for orders from her first instructor. He sensed her anxiety as she waited for his evaluation.

"Sit down, for goodness sake." Ulian shook his head as she complied. "We've worked together for far too long to have you acting like that around me. Don't you think?"

"My apologies. I'm nervous."

"You successfully completed the mission," Ulian replied. "Against disadvantageous odds even. What would you say would be the biggest failure of the operation?"

"Allowing the humans to take the facility," Morala said. "Doing so nearly cost us the primary objective."

Ulian nodded. It wasn't a bad answer. "But ultimately, they pulled it off."

"Yes, but we had no way of knowing that when the Tol'An pulled out."

"What do you think was *your* biggest failure during the mission?"

Morala sighed through her nose, brows furrowing. Clearly, she hadn't considered the question until that moment. "I suppose … I did not offer as much morale as I could've to our people. I should have given them more encouragement, less direct orders. I think I may have been too abrupt in my manner."

"Reason?"

"I was too focused on the end result rather than the journey to get there."

Ulian smiled. "Insightful."

"What rating would you give me?"

"Highly successful," Ulian said. "Congratulations on a job well done. I'm glad that my faith in you was justified."

Morala seemed to relax all at once.

"Are you really so relieved? Did you honestly think I would feel differently?"

"I was concerned," Morala replied. "Because this was an important mission and in the midst of combat, orders are easy to second guess. It felt as if I could've made many mistakes. They seemed wise at the time … our people performed well. But the loss of life when it came to our pilots … I regret that."

"The fighter portion of our military needs to make some adjustments as to how they train them," Ulian said. "That's not necessarily on you or me. But I do understand how you feel. In any event, when we go into hyperspace, we can go through the entire battle together if you'd like some more detailed feedback."

"I would be honored."

"Excellent. Then I would request you to take charge of repairs while I confer with Captain Bradford. I believe he and I should discuss the next operation. We'd like to get that final Orb before dealing with the Tol'An and the sooner we begin, the sooner this conflict can end. Thank you for your time, Morala."

"You as well, sir."

Morala left him alone and he turned his attention to the port hole, staring outside. Space seemed peaceful now that the conflict ended. He looked forward to the time when they weren't hopping between conflicts, battling various enemies but even when the Tol'An were dealt with, there would always be more threats.

Ulian heard rumors of a pirate cartel starting trouble on the trade lanes and some of the old colonies were making noise about their taxes. The military would have need of him for as long as he made himself available. He didn't regret his life, nor the events that honed him into a warrior, but he felt the beginning of exhaustion weighing on his soul.

It'll be time to get out soon, Ulian thought. *But not just yet. Not until the Tol'An are gone and I feel my home is relatively safe. Then ... maybe then, I can step away.* Working with Morala gave him hope for the future. Bright officers like her represented a new generation of soldier for the Pahxin people. If he turned over the reins to her, he knew she'd do a good job.

***

Dala made her way through the Gnosis hangar but had to pause just outside. She had to ask for directions but finally found her way to the medical bay nearly twenty minutes later. There, she found the members of Mustang Squadron gathered around their leader. Approaching quietly, she half expected them to be mourning the man.

Much to her relief, Dennis was sitting up, chatting animatedly about the battle. She smiled, but mastered her emotions, clearing her throat to announce her presence. All eyes fell on her and she lifted her hand in greeting. A couple of the pilots scowled but the one person that mattered returned the gesture.

"Hi Dala," Dennis said. "Thanks for coming to see me."

"I don't have long," Dala replied. "We're all going to hyperspace soon. I received clearance to ensure you were okay. In person. They wanted me to send a com call." She sighed. "My apologies, I don't mean to ramble. I'm … I'm quite pleased to see you up and speaking."

"Thanks to a little effort from the bomber crews." Dennis shrugged. "I wasn't out there long." He looked at the others. "Can we have a moment, guys?"

Dala got the sense they had some words for her, but they kept their opinions to themselves while pacing away. He motioned for her to come closer and she stepped up beside him, clasping his hand. Looking into his eyes, she tried to gauge how he felt, whether he blamed her or not for being shot down.

"We're cool," Dennis said. "Don't worry about it. That kind of thing happens … pilots get shot down. And that was a rough mission."

"I don't know what *cool* means but ... you are ... certain?" Dala tilted her head. "I ... I feel responsible. I'm sorry that I only brought the three of us."

"Alicia was a good call. She told me what happened after I punched out. You guys did great." Dennis shrugged. "And hey, overall objective was completed. We have the Orb and we're on our way home. I'd call that a pretty big win."

"We lost several ..." Dala shook her head. "But not as many as in the past I suppose." She let him go and straightened up. "I'm glad you're not cross with me. I didn't mean for this to happen. You mean something to me. Our time together has been pleasant, and I look forward to more."

Dennis grinned. "If you don't get off this ship soon, you might be spending a lot more time with me." He motioned with his head toward to the door. "The light indicates we're moving toward hyperspace soon."

Dala's eyes widened. "I should go then." She paused, torn with indecision. Finally, she leaned over him and pressed her lips to his forehead. "Rest. We will see each other again when we are back on your planet where I can make this up to you properly. Until then ... farewell, Dennis."

She left the medical bay before he could respond, rushing back toward the hangar. Her heart pounded hard in her chest. The trip from the Stalwart to the Gnosis filled her with dread, terror at having lost his friendship, and whatever else might've been developing between them. He survived ... and miraculously, so did their burgeoning relationship.

After everything else they were doing, all the fighting and rushing to finish off the Tol'An, the simplest of things gave Dala a reason to fight. Protecting her country, her friends and their new allies felt like worthy goals, the kind she willingly risked her life for. Having ensured her newest bond remained strong, a newfound confidence made her hopeful for the future.

Printed in Great Britain
by Amazon